anya and the shy guy

SUZE WINEGARDNER

Entangled Publishing, LLC
2614 South Timberline Road
Suite 109
Fort Collins, CO 80525
Visit our website at www.entangledpublishing.com.

Crush is an imprint of Entangled Publishing, LLC.

Edited by Stephen Morgan
Cover design by Jessica Cantor
Cover art by iStock

Manufactured in the United States of America

First Edition July 2015

For my mum who gave me a love of books,
and my dad who gave me a love of travel.

Preface

WILL FRAY

Age: 18

Hair: Darkish

Eyes: Murky-pond-water gray

Hometown: Jacksonville, Florida

Favorite song on debut album: The One

Turn-ons: Piercings, midnight bus rides, and fried bread

His dream date: A walk in the park, with some illicit making out. Okay, a lot of illicit making out.

Quote to live by: "Ain't no thing like me, 'cept me!"

Rocket, Guardians of the Galaxy

Chapter One

Anya let her battered backpack fall to the floor in the small guard hut at the stadium. She peered again at the letter she'd just been given along with her backstage all-access pass.

"Will Fray?" she whispered, the words crackling in the back of her throat. "I'm assigned to Will Fray? I thought I had access to the whole band." She stopped to clear her throat as her underused vocal chords fritzed.

"What did you say, hon?" The huge, tattooed security man's eyes were glued to his monitors.

She struggled to remember which one Will was. The blond? The one with all the ink?

No. *Now* she remembered him. She pictured a magazine photo of a good-looking guy half hiding behind dark floppy hair. He was the shy one. The one who could barely string a sentence together for the few interviews she'd read. Awesome.

The guard shrugged and pointed to a fleet of buses at

the far side of the parking lot. "Will's over there on the bus. Watch where you walk. There's cables and expensive equipment everywhere. You'll be thrown out of here if you damage anything."

Anya had a nasty feeling that if she left the security hut with the letter it would cement her fate. She cleared her throat again, but her voice still came out in a pathetic whisper. "Who do I talk to about this?" And then her reedy voice found its volume knob and echoed around the mostly empty hut. "I was supposed to be covering the whole band, but they only seem to have given me access to one of them."

This was not cool. Not cool at all. Fear of failure gripped her, pressing down on her chest as she tried to take an even breath. She really didn't want to pass out this close to the jackpot.

He heaved a sigh. "The person you need to speak to is S2J's manager, LJ. But I wouldn't if I were you. I'd suck it up and keep out of his way. Just a friendly piece of advice." He sat back down and turned his attention to the security monitors.

Frustration burned behind her eyes, and she kept her face as straight as she could. She'd learned from living on the street that tears didn't make anything better. Tears were only useful if you needed food or the odd dollar. She wasn't going to waste them on the security man or this boy band.

But still, she'd accepted the job so that she could try to dig up some exclusive dirt on one of the band members in the hope that it could earn her a big enough payday to get off the streets and back to school. And get Jude the help he needed. She had to keep that at the front of her mind.

Money. I'm here for the money. The money that can make

me safe. Make us *safe.*

Jude had saved her life when she'd first become homeless. Literally. An older man—a veteran, judging by his tattoos, he'd never said so himself—he had his own demons that kept him on the streets. And now, finally, she was in a position to help him for a change. She could *not* blow this. She wasn't going to let him down.

She picked up her backpack, trying to appear casual, instead of the total mess of anxiety that was her default state of being, and made her way through the elaborate row of gates and fences designed to keep the fans away from the band.

Girls were five deep trying to get a glimpse of the world-famous boys. Homemade posters hung on the metal bars, and for a second she wondered how much she could sell her all-access pass for. Since she'd been assigned to Will Fray, the quietest guy in the band, that might actually be her best money-making option.

Jeez. Just one break. Please.

Except this *was* her break, and she was going to make it work. Or die trying.

She hauled her backpack onto one shoulder and, by habit, patted the pocket that held her notebook. Check. With no cell phone and no laptop she relied on her notebook to record every conversation, every interview, every idea.

It was that attention to detail that had gotten her this gig. WowSounds.com had been so impressed with the authenticity of her article on the homeless of Tulsa that they'd asked her to pick up Seconds to Juliet's *Make it Last* tour here. They'd never suspected she was, in fact, one of the people she'd "interviewed" for that piece. They'd also never suspected she was only seventeen.

"You all right, miss?"

She turned back to the security guard who had come out of his hut. "Are the fans here every day?"

His gaze flittered over the throng of girls. "Since we arrived in town, yeah. They're not allowed to go speak to them. The boys I mean."

"Why's that?"

"LJ thinks that once the girls get a photo and an auto-graph, they won't bother buying the albums or coming to the concerts."

"Is that true? I would've thought it would make them want to see them more."

"Me, too. But what do I know? I'm just the muscle." He took her by the shoulders, turned her back around, and pointed her in the direction of the buses.

She stiffened under his touch but tried not to react. He pushed her lightly. "Leave your luggage at the bus, and then someone will show you around."

"Thanks." She headed off across the lot, sweat trickling down her back. She mentally went over the very few articles she'd read about Will Fray. She'd have to look at her notes as soon as she found somewhere safe and quiet to work.

She'd spent the last two days researching at the library she'd always used to send her articles in to the editor. Her notebook was filled with the songs, albums, quotes, and background info on all the guys.

This would have been so much easier if she had access to the whole band. Out of all of them, Ryder was the one most likely to have some dark secret she could expose. He was the bad boy. Instead, she was stuck with Will Fray.

Magazines had dubbed him the "shy one," but as far as she was concerned, he may as well be the "boring one."

What did girls even see in him? She was sure he was cute and all, but she liked boys who weren't afraid to speak their mind. The chances of him giving her any kind of info to work with were probably next to none. Zero. Nothing.

She stopped dead and looked at the bus in front of her.

Were they for real? The freaking tour bus had a huge decal of the band with no shirts on. She pushed up her cheap sunglasses and took a long look. She couldn't take her eyes off it.

It was cheesy, campy, and made her stomach feel weird. She rubbed her belly for a second and then took a quick look around to make sure no one was watching her. She sneaked her small digital camera out of a pocket and took a quick snap. She pressed down the five-year-old Hello Kitty sticker on the camera and peered again at the picture on the side of the bus.

Hmm. Will must be one of these half-naked guys. She wished she could remember exactly which one. Though she had to admit, all of them looked pretty good.

Here goes nothing.

Anya took a breath, smoothed down her choppy, pinned-up hair and knocked on the bus door. Music boomed from inside the bus, and she rolled her eyes to herself. They were listening to their own music on their own tour bus? She couldn't wait to slip that nugget into her story. Could they *be* further up their own butts?

This time she knocked with her whole fist, rattling the door. The music went silent. Thank God for small mercies.

• • •

Matt didn't care how much fun movies made it seem for twins to switch places. This was anything but fun.

I wish I wasn't here.

I wish Will was here.

Twin swaps were not as much fun when you were over the age of eight. It wasn't *The Parent Trap* anymore, it was more like *The Shining*.

He flipped the page of his notebook full of S2J song lyrics and skipped over "The One"—maybe their most popular song to date. He already knew the words to virtually all the songs, especially that one…hell, everyone in the effing western hemisphere knew the lyrics to that one.

Better for him to focus on the couple of songs that tripped him up every time he rotated to backing vocals. Luckily, the fans just screamed the whole way through the set, so no one ever noticed him screwing up the words. But someone would eventually, which meant he'd better figure out the songs fast. He'd come too far to let his twin down now.

A loud banging at the door shook the whole freaking bus.

What the…?

He stomped over and swung it open, forcing the visitor back down the steps.

Well hell-o, sunshine.

Except there was nothing sunshiny about her at all. She was all rich black hair and a pissed off expression. Her hair had a row of tiny hair grips, like little kid ones with cartoon characters and small flowers, which didn't distract him at all from her eyes. Gray and blue and...unforgiving.

Geez. He'd hate to be the one who crossed her.

A tiny ring decorated her left eyebrow. So she had a hint of dangerous, too. He didn't know if he was insanely attracted to her or just scared of her. But there was something else in those eyes. Some kind of wariness or sadness or something.

I wonder what her secret is...

"Can I help you?"

"I'm beginning to doubt it, but I was told that I'm stuck with you for two weeks." She dropped her backpack to the ground, and it looked so heavy it must have had her whole life in it. "You are Will Fray, aren't you?"

He kept his eyes on her hands, as he'd been drilled to. Not in case she had a gun, but in case she whipped her top off. It happened. A lot. And their prick of a manager had warned them that a photo with a topless teenager would get them kicked out of the band faster than a missed stage cue. Fortunately, her hands remained at her side.

"Maybe. Why are you stuck with me?" He scanned the parking lot for the nonexistent security. Typical.

Her eyes sparkled a little as she thrust a letter at him. It was from LJ, the prick of a manager, telling this girl—he looked at the name it was addressed to—Anya Anderson, that she was assigned to Will Fray for two whole weeks to write an article for WowSounds.com.

Matt's blood ran cold.

Bastard.

He'd seen that LJ was a little suspicious of him, had seen the odd looks he gave him when they were onstage, but this was a nightmare. How could he keep his brother's secret if he had to be Will 24/7?

He tried for a smile. "I guess you *are* stuck with me."

"Well now that that's settled…" She started to climb up the steps to the bus.

He held up his hand. "No, no, no. Just no. Stop right there. Only the band is allowed on this bus. You get to ride on the hangers-on bus."

Her eyes narrowed at his dis, and the wave of shade coming from her was overwhelming. Shit. One way to make sure she dug deep until she found out his secrets was to piss her off.

Charm her, idiot.

"I meant the Hanging On bus," he said. "All the buses on tour are named after the songs from our first album. This bus"—he gestured behind him—"is called The One."

She stepped back and looked at the side of the bus. He cringed. His one saving grace was that it wasn't actually *his* half-naked body on the photo, it was his twin's. But she didn't know that. And come on. He might spend a little more time in the gym than Will, but at the end of the day, they were twins. Same genetics. Same body.

She cocked her head. "Are you sure it's not called Not Tonight?"

He laughed. At least she had the band's discography down. "Nope. Not Tonight is the name of the chaperones' bus. The one with the shitty suspension is called the Rock You bus."

"Dare I ask who rides on the Kiss This bus?" she asked with a completely straight face.

"I couldn't possibly divulge that kind of private stuff without knowing you better. Much better."

This girl. He had to give it to her, she wasn't like the other journalists he'd avoided thus far. He might even be okay with a little up-close-and-personal time with…what was her name again? Anya?

She paused and tipped her head to one side. "You're not as shy as you make yourself out to be, are you?"

His smile fell from his face.

Nice one, Matt. Don't forget you *have a secret to hide. Distract, distract.*

"Don't believe everything you read, baby, everything you see, baby, I can be your everything, baby…" He winced. Crap. What possessed him to quote his brother's lyrics? He'd been doing so well pretending to be Will, and three seconds with this Anya person had thrown him off his game.

"Really? Does that actually work? Quoting your own lyrics at girls?" She looked almost embarrassed for him, pitying, even.

"I'm—I'm sorry," he deliberately stammered, trying to channel Will's shyness. "I—I just liked, *like* the way you look." Jesus. Even Will would have come up with something smoother than that.

She peered awkwardly down at her thick black tights, jean shorts, and holey T-shirt. "Now I know you're lying. I like that. That's actually a good start." She took a thick notebook from a pocket of the bag and hauled her backpack onto her shoulder. She uncapped a pen with her mouth and nodded. "A very good start."

Crap.

Chapter Two

As soon as she heard the trailer door shut behind her, Anya stopped and held her shaking hand out in front of her. It trembled as if she'd just witnessed a murder. She fisted it and took a deep breath. Even her inhale was unsteady. She'd forgotten how long it had been since she'd looked someone in the eye. Since she'd spoken to someone her age. Since she'd felt interested in anything beyond finding a safe place to sleep.

Two years ago, she'd woken up alone in the house to the sound of the bailiff hammering on the front door, and ever since then, she'd been pretty much on her own. Okay, there'd been *one* foster home, but three days there had been all it took for her to figure being murdered on the streets would be preferable to another night under that roof.

Survival meant staying invisible. Not being noticed.

Except Will had noticed her.

It was her own fault. She'd been so aggressive with him.

But what else was she supposed to do when he talked to her like that? He was just begging for a nice verbal lashing.

She had to be careful. It was amazing she'd gotten this far as it was.

She was lucky WowSounds.com liked her writing enough that they hadn't dug too deeply into who she was. She'd written that one piece on the homeless—never divulging that she knew so much because she *was* homeless. They'd sent a check for $50 to a friendly grocery shop owner, who'd cashed it for her. She'd then written a feature piece about being homeless on the streets of Tulsa, which had garnered $250 and a request to spend two weeks with the band.

WowSounds.com had no idea she was seventeen. She may have even led them to believe that she was a married mother. Another lie. But one that seemed to warm them toward her. Add one more knot to the tangled net in her stomach.

She found the Hanging On bus—not that hard since the name was emblazoned down the side—and knocked on the door.

It flew open with a bang, and a young woman stared down at her. A grin immediately spread across her face. "You must be Anya Anderson. Come on in." She stepped back inside the bus and disappeared from view.

Anya took the few steps up into the darkness and tried to keep up. It was like another world in there. All the windows had blinds drawn and spotlights hit beige leather seats, sofas, and booths.

The woman was talking as she caught up with her. "It's just us on this bus. There are six bunks—look. I took the one at the end, hope you don't mind. I won't be here much, though. I have family in town and they're all staying at a fancy hotel downtown, so I'll be visiting them mostly. Pick a bunk." She chattered at about a hundred miles an hour, her long dark hair swinging with every step and almost every word.

The sleeping section was unlit, and each bunk had a curtain. She pulled one back and looked inside. They were pretty big beds, with a storage unit above them, and a TV in the wall at the foot of the bed. They were two by two, and the lower bunk seemed to have slightly more room to sit up in bed, so she slid her backpack off her shoulders and fought back a fizzing in the back of her eyes. She would have a bed tonight. Her fingers fluttered over the soft sheets. It was a real bed.

"Are you okay?" the woman asked.

No sense in being truthful. Instead she stuck out her hand. "I'm Anya."

The wide grin made a reappearance. "I'm Natasha. I work makeup when Deb's off. God bless the union, right? No more working three hundred days in a row, right? What do you do?"

"I'm writing about the band. Will Fray, I mean. I guess." Anya pulled the curtain back over her bunk. "Will my stuff be safe here?"

"Sure. No one comes on this bus. It's not as fancy as the others. I've been sharing it on and off since I got here. Daisy usually stays here, too. She's Trevin's girlfriend, but she's at home for a couple of weeks. All her stuff is still here, though, on that top bed at the end." She gave Anya a once-over and raised her eyebrows. "You're a writer? You look really young to be a writer. How old are you? The package that came was addressed to Mrs. Anya Anderson. Are you married?"

Sweet hell. It took Anya a couple of seconds to unravel all her questions. "I'm nineteen. I guess they must have made a mistake. I'm not married." *Diversion. Diversion. Need a diversion.* "What package?" she countered.

"It's in the galley. Kitchen. Whatever. I think the return address was from WowSounds. Is that who you work for?" Natasha slumped into an armchair and swung her legs over the arm. "Nineteen? You have fabulous skin. I'd love to work on you sometime."

Anya turned the package between her hands. What had they sent her?

"Aren't you going to open it?" Natasha asked.

Anya took some scissors out of a knife block on the Formica counter top. She looked at them for a second. They were like the ones her mom had given her to cut out paper dolls. She remembered the scissors, but she'd blocked out a lot of other stuff about her mom. How tall she was, how she spoke. Even her face. Well, her nice face, anyway. Not the drugged-out face. That one she'd probably never forget.

She cut into the tape. "How old are you?" she asked. Offense was the best defense, after all.

"Twenty-three, but don't tell. They think I'm twenty-five. LJ instigated a new rule about the age of females on the tour. All the younger girls who've joined the tour for one reason or another have hooked up with the guys in the band. LJ does *not* like that."

"Why?"

Natasha smiled, like she knew something no one else knew. "The band members are all supposed to be single and available. The new cutoff date for people of the female persuasion is twenty-five so, for God's sake, steer clear of LJ. There's no way he'll believe you're older than nineteen. No offense. You'd be kicked off the tour faster than a fan's separated from her panties." She swung her legs so they kicked in time to the music playing in the background that Anya hadn't noticed.

"Why did you tell me your real age? I mean, if anyone finds out, won't you be fired?"

"Yeah. But you can keep a secret, can't you?"

Anya barely suppressed a chuckle. She smiled and nodded.

"Then we're both fine. You have to take a leap of faith with a new friend, right? Especially when you're on tour. We all become like family. And since we're sharing bunks, we're family." She spoke like that had been settled. They were friends. Family, even. Period.

Anya's heart fluttered with the prospect of having a girlfriend she could trust. But she also made a mental note *not* to go speak to this LJ man about only being given access to Will. She couldn't blow this. She just needed to make the best of it.

She peeled some plastic wrapping away from a tablet computer. It was heavily branded with WowSounds, and it was scuffed around the edges, making her think that it had been used before.

The note was from the editor, Cynthia.

Mrs. Anderson. Wanted you to have this, as it has a shared drive. Just use this to file your daily blog posts and then the final wrap-up article, and there's no need to send them, and no chance they'll get lost. I hope to see you soon.

Good luck,

Cynthia Wilcox,

Editor-at-large.

WowSounds.com

Cool. She'd been a little anxious about sneaking away to the local library to file her stories, and she'd had visions of the tour leaving town while she was trying to upload her posts on the virtually antique computers. She'd even thought through asking to borrow someone's computer.

One knot released in her stomach. Maybe this was a good sign.

Those words at the end of the letter, though…

I hope to see you soon.

Hopefully that was just a sign-off and not a specific plan. Anya couldn't actually meet her. God, wouldn't *that* be a catastrophe?

"Do you want me to show you around?" Natasha jumped up, as if sitting for a few minutes was too boring to do any longer. "I warn you, there's not much to do here. Everyone's usually napping during the day, because Lord knows we're up till the early hours most nights." She led Anya out of the bus and down the steps.

Natasha described the inhabitants of each bus as they walked down the long line of them snaking along the edge of a private parking lot of the arena. As they passed The One, Anya couldn't help but notice a guy disappearing through the door she had been banned from. He must be one of the other members of Seconds to Juliet. One of the guys she'd been forbidden from covering. She rubbernecked a little to see if she could match his face to the image on the side of the bus. Unfortunately he was gone too fast.

• • •

Matt relaxed when Trevin entered the bus. He was the only person here who knew his secret. Knew about Will.

"How's he doing?" Trevin asked as he sat on one of the leather armchairs.

"He's doing good," Matt replied. He never knew what to say to that question. Will trusted Trevin, because they'd become closer during the tour, but Matt didn't know him well enough. If he admitted that Will was still in rehab, that he was finding it painful to deal with his injury without drugs, would Trevin use that information somehow?

"I'm glad to hear it," Trevin said. "It's not the same without Will. I mean, you're close, but not the real thing, you know?"

Ain't that the truth. "I do know." Matt laughed. He might not know Trevin very well, but he couldn't help but like him. "What do you need?" He poured a cup of coffee from the carafe and held the cup up in the silent *You want some?* gesture.

Trevin shook his head. "What I need is for you to stop singing 'I'll wash your back' when it should be 'I'll watch your back.' You might not think anyone can hear you, but I can hear you, and you can bet your ass that LJ can hear you, too."

Matt leaned against the counter. *Huh.*

"Well that certainly makes more sense given the rest of the lyrics." He pulled open a drawer and dug the songbook Will had written for him. *Bastard.* "Sorry, dude. The little bastard wrote 'I'll wash your back'. He always did love messing with me."

Trevin grabbed the book and read through it. "Hey, we can give him the benefit of the doubt. He *was* in pain when he wrote this for you. Give me a pen."

Matt chucked him a pencil, and Trevin started scribbling in the book. Shit. It looked like he'd been singing the wrong words to a bunch of songs. No wonder Trevin had stopped by to *check up* on him.

They would just have to make the best of the situation until Will came back. No one could have predicted any of this.

When Will tore his ACL while rehearsing for the tour, LJ had pumped him full of pain-killers so he could continue the tour. One night he'd appeared crying and shivering on their mom's doorstep in Florida, begging for help. LJ's attorney had sent him a letter telling him that if he quit the tour to go to rehab, he'd be in breach of his contract and be sued for $20m. Or rather, their mom would be sued.

One haircut later, with a songbook and an evening of rehearsals in their garage, Matt was on tour, and Will was in rehab. That'd been three weeks ago, and if he was being honest, Matt was still trying to keep his crap together as much as Will. Answering when someone called Will's name. Trying to keep up with dance moves and lyrics. It was hell. But a hell he had to bear to keep his family out of the shit with LJ.

A few more weeks and they could change back, and no one would be the wiser. Matt could head off to college, just like he planned. He dragged his hands over his face. This was probably the biggest and most dangerous scam in the world, and he was in the thick of it.

Winning meant he and his twin could get their lives back. Losing meant he'd be in debt and probably homeless forever. Hell, it could destroy the whole band if any of this came out.

"That should do it. You might want to go through this before tonight's performance." He handed back the book.

Matt took it. "Did you hear that LJ has paired me up with a reporter for two weeks? She arrived today brandishing this." He handed over the letter.

Trevin read it. "Shit. He'd only do this if he was on to you. Wouldn't he?"

"I don't know, man. She's from WowSounds, so it must be legit." He sipped his lukewarm coffee and looked out of the one-way window. If she was shadowing him, he'd have to be even more "on" than before. Maybe that was part of LJ's plan. "Do you think he suspects?"

LJ did have some incentive to sic a reporter on him, though, didn't he? When the band had been brand new, LJ had agreed to take them on if they all signed a share deal that made him the sixth member of the band. Everyone got an equal share. But if any of them dropped out, LJ would get their share, too.

"No. Well, I don't know. He wouldn't risk saying anything unless he was 100 percent sure. But you know he wants Will's share, so this might be his way of either pressuring Will into falling off the wagon, or…"

"…just firing me because I'm Matt, right? Shit."

At the time it had been a good deal, because frankly the band needed the five-time platinum-disc-winning manager more than he needed them.

But now?

Now Matt and Trevin wondered if he had deliberately set Will up for failure. He would beat the shit out of LJ if he could. But he couldn't, not while their manager had so much power over them.

Keep your head down and play the game. Four more weeks until Will gets out of rehab, give or take...

Trevin got up. "Don't worry. I'll get you both through this. Just...stay cool, don't fuck with LJ, and for God's sake, charm this reporter. Make her like you. Be onstage in ten, okay?"

"Sure. Thanks, man." They fist-bumped like bosses, and then Trevin left the bus the same way he'd come in: with a slammed door.

Matt took a breath and held his hand in front of him. It shook a little. Not as much as last week, though.

Chapter Three

Anya took a breath and raised her hand to knock on the door. She'd just met LJ. She'd tried not to, but he'd appeared when Natasha had been showing her the makeup trailer. They'd just backed out of the bus to avoid two girls who were in there getting their makeup done. Afterward, Natasha had explained that they were S2J's opening act and that Anya shouldn't cross paths with them if she could help it.

She was okay with that. She very definitely wanted to stay out of trouble. If anyone looked really hard at her for any reason, she could be busted from the tour, busted from WowSounds, and back on the street before she could scream "S2J".

As Natasha was about to dish the dirt on the two girls, they'd run into LJ. He'd narrowed his eyes at her and ordered her back to Will Fray's side. Told her not to let him out of her sight. She'd stammered a "Yessir" and bolted back to find Will. At least he'd bought her age. Probably. Maybe he had. She wasn't sure. She knew she looked a bit older than she was so that helped, but he'd still looked at her with a decent amount of suspicion. Damn. Running into him like that had been worse than that one time those drunk college guys had chased her. She'd known the streets better than them and had managed to lose them eventually. But LJ. He was a whole new level of scary. Mostly because he had the power to kick her out. And she had to stay there. For Jude.

She dropped her hand and stepped back off the bus steps. Inhale. Exhale. Her hands shook even as she clenched them. She was safe. Inhale. Exhale. No one could hurt her here. She just had to figure out a way to stay on the tour, and stay out of trouble, until she found her story.

She looked back at Will's door. It had been so long since anyone had spoken to her. Really spoken to her. Looked her in the eye.

Today had already been overwhelming. And as much as she wanted to—oh my God did she want to—get off the streets and go to school or get a job, right at this moment she wanted to be back out there. Alone and anonymous. Curled up and not having to talk to anyone. It was dangerous on the streets, but at least there, she knew how to keep herself safe. She had no idea how to survive here.

Come on, you can do this.

She took one last breath and stomped up the three steps loudly, banging her flat palm against the door as soon as she reached it.

Take no prisoners.

The door snapped open and she grabbed onto the rail to stop herself from stumbling down the steps.

"What? Oh it's you." Will squinted a little like he'd just

woken up. "Hi." He overcompensated with a huge grin. A worryingly manic one.

Weird.

"Mr... Um, I mean LJ told me I had to stick to you like glue." She shrugged apologetically. "So here I am. Being sticky." *Being sticky?*

His smile faltered, leaving a furrowed brow for a split second. Then it was gone, and a slightly smoother grin took its place. "Yes you are. Here, that is. And I guess we'll just have to see how sticky you are. I'm heading to a quick rehearsal onstage. Do you want to come?" He held out his hand as if she was a little girl.

Anya couldn't help but bristle. "According to LJ, I have to come." She stepped back to allow him to lead the way and ignored his hand. It dropped to his side as he turned toward the huge stadium. Just because he was some superstar, it didn't mean he could be condescending to her like that. She wanted to be really annoyed, but she couldn't help wonder what it would have felt like if she'd taken his hand. How long would he have held it for? Who would have been the first to let go?

Will interrupted her thoughts. "We kind of fucked up this one song last night. One of the guys nearly slid off the stage, so we're trying to figure out how to ensure we finish the set without a death in the band. Hopefully it shouldn't take too long." He led her through zigzagging metal barriers, doors where they had to show their passes, until they got inside the stadium.

The football field had been covered with wooden flooring and rows and rows of seats. A prickle went up her spine as she absorbed the size of the venue This band must be a lot more popular than she'd imagined. She never knew so many people could see one band at the same time.

Then the lights came on with a bang and the whole stage and arena were flooded with a white light. The enormity of what she had done descended on her.

"Sit a few rows back if you don't want to get wet," Will said as he jumped over two rows of barriers and pulled himself onto the stage.

Wait…what did he just say?

The buzzing of the lights echoed around the empty seats. She followed him to the front and stood at the barrier, watching as he leaned on a speaker and checked his phone.

Who would he have an email or text from that wasn't already here? Did he have friends? A girlfriend? Was he looking at the financial pages of an online newspaper? She snorted at the thought as she sat down. *Yeah, right.* But these were the things she had to find out for her article.

Panic settled in her stomach as if it were renting a space and bringing in furniture. This was a huge band. Not some small-time small-town band that might make it big. And she had pretended to be in her twenties to get this gig. To report on the band. And she had no idea how she was supposed to interview them, or what was really expected of her. She'd effed up royally. And this was huge. She took a deep breath which did little to quell the tension rising in her.

A loud chord blared out of the speakers, and then a few single notes. Then it went silent again.

"Sorry, just finding the right place," someone shouted from behind her.

She craned her head and saw a man with headphones standing on a platform in the middle of the seated area. He looked older. Friendly.

What kind of secrets did he have in his back pocket? Hell, what kind of secrets did all of the stagehands and roadies have about the band? They'd probably seen things no one would believe.

A plan started to formulate in her mind. Maybe she could write nightly blog posts for WowSounds from the perspectives of the ordinary people on the tour, and then she could do the longer interviews with Will every other day or so. Maybe she could get questions from the readers to ask Will during the day.

She whipped out her notebook and started to take notes.

By the time she looked up, satisfied that she had figured out a way to manage this without messing it up, music was playing and four other guys were on the stage getting miked up by a man who had his own headset on.

It seemed that they used head mikes, so they didn't have to hold an actual microphone. In turn four of them said, "Testing, one two, one two," into the microphone, and their voices bounced around the stadium like they were in some kind of echo chamber.

The last guy wore a black T-shirt that showed off a bunch of tattoos. He said, "Fuck this shit, fuck this shit," in the same way the others had done their sound check. Satisfied, he gave a thumbs-up to the sound guys. She guessed that was Ryder, the Bad Boy.

Anya smiled to herself, but the guys onstage looked anything but amused. Was there tension here? Oh God, she hoped so. She wanted to blow the lid off something that could earn her decent money.

She huddled over her messenger bag and pulled her feet

up to the seat. The lights went out and a groaning piece of stage equipment, like a huge arch, eased forward on tracks to the front of the stage. It stopped over the boys who were standing in a line, shifting from foot to foot as if they were anxious to get it over with.

Spotlights flicked on as the music started. The beats vibrated through Anya's body, and she realized how unique it was to be watching a band as the only person in the audience. Will started to sing, but she could barely make out the words as his voice reverberated around her. Then the others harmonized, and she started to get into it.

She'd never heard this song before, but where would she have? She did all her band research at the library, where it was definitely frowned upon to have music blaring from the computer speakers. Her head bobbed to the bass line, and a smile crept across her face. It was good. Who would have thought?

And then they stopped singing, someone shouted at someone else, and in a split second, they were shoving each other and yelling. What had she missed? The backing track ground to a halt, and LJ ran onstage and held a mike to the speaker. The feedback whine was so loud, Anya swore they could have heard it in Atlanta. Then he spoke.

"What the fuck are you doing? If you can't be professional in front of a fucking reporter"—he pointed at Anya—"then I will send you back to the little town piss pots you came from, unnerstand?" He didn't wait for a reply, just threw the mike at their feet and stalked off the stage.

Whoa. Do not get on his wrong side. Do not get caught lying to him about my age. Or anything.

• • •

It was always Ryder who couldn't keep it together. What was up with him? Matt wished that he'd interrogated Will about the personalities in the band as much as he had the music. He just didn't get most of them. Maybe Ryder was pissed because his girl Mia was out of town for a couple of weeks.

There was silence as LJ left the stage. As much as Matt hated him, he couldn't entirely blame him for being pissed at the constant sniping and barely concealed agitation between the band members. When they said in interviews that they were like one big family, it was this agitation and frustration that they were referring to. According to Will, it hadn't always been this way. They were tight friends, and would do anything for one another, but the intense time they spent together sometimes fueled petty disputes and arguments that thankfully usually ended in laughs and the busting of chops.

"All right, let's hit this one again, shall we?" Trevin asked with fake politeness. That guy sometimes seemed to have the weight of the world on him, as well as Will and Matt's problems.

Although no one said a word in response to his request, everyone assumed their starting positions again without complaint. The music gave them their cue, and Matt started to sing, channeling his twin with every inflection. He might get the words wrong here and there—no thanks to Will— but Trevin had been right about one thing. Matt was getting closer to Will's sound.

As the others joined in, the song got faster, until it was almost a rap. Then, at the climax, there was a pause, sound effects of thunder and lightning flashed, and then the rain came.

That was where it almost always went wrong. The rain machine opened up on them as they segued back into the sultry opening of the song. They sang as they got soaked. And in the last chorus of the song, they did what drove all the girls crazy.

They did a few dance steps in sync. Synchronized dance steps weren't their thing at all. But in the last chorus of the last song, they went for it.

If the crowd had voices left, they screamed at the sight of them doing their dance under the shower. Ryder nearly always ripped off his shirt at the end. Sometimes one of the other guys did, too. But Matt couldn't. *Too much to hide.*

As finales went, though, this was hard to beat. They just had to finish without injuring themselves, like Will had done.

The stage was slippery when wet, and even some of the rubber stripping was a deathtrap if your feet got stuck to it, or if, in Will's case, it had peeled off in the middle, making a loop that he'd caught his foot in, wrenching his knee.

It was a huge hazard, but no one had come up with a more impactful way to end the show. They took their last dance step, which was kicking the water into the front row of the audience. Actually the rain machine flicked up at the same time, which made the front rows feel like they were getting wet from the stage water. "Trevin got my T-shirt wet" merchandise went for a minimum of $50 on eBay. But here, they were really getting hosed by the machine. He tried to see the reporter-girl, but the "rain" decreased visibility. He wondered what she thought of the number.

After the last note of the backing track faded, the spots

clanged off and the stage lights came back on. There was nothing like nailing a song in rehearsal to put everyone in a good mood, even Ryder, so they bumped fists and laughed together as they waited for the okay to leave from the choreographer, Moses.

"Okay, guys, that looked good," Moses said. "I think the diagonal rubber tape seems to provide less of a trip hazard now. You all okay with that?" He nodded as they all affirmed. "Okay, you're done for the day. There's a meeting tomorrow morning at ten a.m. sharp to go over the last details of your appearance and script changes for Tulsa. After that, you have free time until six p.m. Then it's makeup and stage-wait until showtime. Now get lost, all of you." He grinned as he dismissed them.

Matt jumped off the stage and made his way to whassername. Shit, he couldn't believe he'd already forgotten her name. She was huddled in the front row, hair soaked and T-shirt clinging to—he swallowed hard—every part of her. "Shit, I'm sorry. I told you to stay out of the front row."

"I didn't hear you. And by the time I figured out what you'd said, I was already mentally figuring out how to build an ark." She blew a heavy wet strand of jet-black hair from her face. As her gray eyes met his, he immediately remembered her name: Anya.

Anya. A silence fell as her name ran through his head, backward and forward, until it became a part of his regular vocabulary. Like "water," and "air," and "sexy as hell."

What? Out of all the girls I've met since becoming "Will," I get the hots for the one here to dig up our secrets.

Great going, Matt. Great.

"Just call me Noah," she said as if she was reading his

mind, the way his twin sometimes did.

He recovered his train of thought and laughed, relieved that she had such a great sense of humor. "If it's any consolation, I'm a lot wetter than you, and I have to do this nearly every evening, whether it's eighty degrees out or forty."

She frowned. "Dude, you're in the South. It's never going to be forty degrees here."

Busted. "True. I was really going for the sympathy vote." He shrugged and grinned, heartened to see that she was grinning back.

"I'm not one for the sympathy vote. I vote practical all day long." She stuffed her wet notebook into her wet bag and stood up.

"Good to know. And on that practical note, we should change into some dry clothes."

"No kidding." Her smile had gone, and right there, he knew he'd do anything to see that mischievous grin again.

Dammit. Get a grip.

Diversion. Quick.

"Hey, if you're writing about us, don't mention any details about the number you just saw us rehearse," he said. "It's the finale, and although people can't help but post photos of it, we try not to mention the specifics…just to maybe surprise the people who aren't on the fan sites."

"Well it certainly surprised me. No problem. I won't mention it," she said.

Suddenly he pictured her totally wet, dripping from the rain or the shower. Her hair down, a real smile on her face, just for him. Water running down her shoulders, maybe clumping her eyelashes together…

Clumping her…? Jesus, Matt. Shut up, you wimp.

"What are you thinking about?" she asked.

"The homeless shelter we're going to tomorrow," he lied. "We're hoping to raise the profile of the place to show people that they need more public housing in the city. We're also donating money to the organization that supports getting the homeless back to work." *Yup, I'm going to hell.* "You'll be there, I guess. If LJ has told you to stick to me like glue." He grinned at her as they stopped at his bus. "Meet you back here in ten?"

"Sure," she said, although she didn't look happy at all.

Oh come the fuck on. How could you not be charmed by a charity-loving superstar?

Except in real life he was neither of those things.

Shit.

Chapter Four

Shit. She'd been to almost all the homeless shelters in Tulsa. They knew her there. How could she get out of going with the band and not be thrown off the tour? The anxiety she'd quashed while watching the rehearsal reared its ugly head and was making out with the panic that was decorating the space it had taken in her stomach.

Or was that hunger? She wasn't sure her body knew how to register hunger anymore. A book in the library had said that if a body went without food, it could forget to alert the brain that it was hungry. Sometimes she'd gone without eating for days and not even thought about it.

She shrugged out of her wet clothes and draped them on one of the curtain rods that gave the bunks some privacy. Since it was only her and Natasha in here, she'd used the one next to her bunk. Carefully, she opened her backpack all the way and looked at the clothes carefully washed, folded, and rolled, all in order of color and warmth. This bag was the one tiny area of her life that she had complete control over. To Anya, it was a thing of beauty. Everything she needed in its own space. She gently extracted a pink T-shirt, her jean skirt, and a pair of flip-flops. She peeked into the tiny bathroom and used two old hair clips to pin back the worst of the wet bangs.

She looked in the mirror, but she didn't see herself. She saw Will onstage. She couldn't believe she got to talk to someone who looked so good. He didn't have the confidence of the others, but she guessed that was why they called him the Shy Guy. He seemed nice. Normal even. Cute. Fun, too.

A butterfly fluttered in her stomach when she thought of him standing in front of her, completely wet like he'd been caught in a rainstorm, looking as if he was going to whisk her off, rescue her from a castle, pull her onto a huge white horse. *Whoa, there, sister. Keep your eyes on the prize, not on his pretty face.*

She pulled herself together. She was here for a reason. An important one. And she wasn't going to be swayed by a cute guy who looked like heaven.

Before she left, she spun the ring in her eyebrow. It was her call to action. Her reminder that the way *she* looked, the way she'd *chosen* to look, was designed as protection. Protection from prying eyes. Protection from people who thought she might be an easy victim. And protection from well-meaning people who wanted to get involved in her life.

She slipped out of the bus with her notebook and pen and walked past three trailers until she reached the band's vehicle. Just as she was about to knock, Will came down the stairs, still buttoning his shirt. For a second all she could see was his broad chest, and her breath hitched. He was tan and smooth, with an evident beginning to a six-pack.

Get a grip, Anya.

Her reaction scared her a little, but she didn't want fear to join forces with panic and anxiety. Two out of the three was quite enough, thank you.

"I thought we'd hit the greenroom. I'm pretty hungry. You?" he asked.

"I could eat," she said carefully, wondering what a greenroom was. Obviously somewhere there was food, at least. She cursed herself for not bringing her bag. She always tried to doggie-bag as many meals as she could whenever she found some. Eat what was going to spoil first, and save the rest for later.

Would she have to pay to eat anything in the greenroom? Or would it be free? She dropped back a pace and checked Will's perfectly formed ass. Nope, he didn't have a wallet with him. So he wasn't paying for anything. But then, he was a rock star.

Free food would be an unbelievable bonus. But it also reminded her of the homeless shelter where she'd tended to get most of her meals.

Crap. The homeless shelter. They were going there tomorrow. What if someone recognized her?

"In here." This time Will just grabbed her hand and led her through a door and along a warren of corridors in the stadium. The place smelled damp like the old waterworks she'd once called her home. For a few weeks at least. She passed a door sign that said Visiting Team Lockers. Ah, that's why the smell was so bad. Football changing rooms.

Will still hadn't let go of her, and she hadn't snatched her hand back. What was wrong with her? She pretended to stumble and pulled free to grab a doorframe.

He looked around with concern. "Are you okay?"

"Yup." She straightened, smiled, and tucked her hand in her skirt pocket. Suddenly she felt off balance, as if she wanted to hold his hand again. But before she could figure out what the hell was going on with her head, he ducked through a door.

"Here we are."

She swore he almost moaned as he said the words, as if he hadn't been fed in days. A man in black pants and a starched white shirt was hovering over the food, moving a plate an inch this way, turning a bowl that way. Anya watched in fascination. So. Much. Food.

There were hundreds of small sandwiches, peeled and sliced fruit, strips of vegetables around various dips, potato chips, and bread. "If you want hot food, there're menus on the tables," Will said, scooping up a handful of chips.

Unable to speak, she picked up one of the menus and looked at it, unseeing. Her eyes prickled with unshed tears. She hadn't seen this much ordinary food in years. Years. Soup, stew, and rice she'd seen a lot of at the city church kitchens that fed the homeless. But food arranged like this, like it was art, was so alien to her, her stomach almost rebelled. Almost.

She placed the menu back on the table and turned to the buffet again. She reached for a piece of melon and snatched her hand back. Could she? She looked at Will, who nodded with a bewildered look. She tried to restrain herself. Really she did.

In seconds, she was tasting a ham sandwich. The grainy mustard made her taste buds tingle, and she moaned. Next was a slice of pineapple, a strawberry. The juiciness flooded her mouth as if the sugar had set off an explosion. She took some chips and a hunk of French bread.

"Jesus. How hungry were you?" Will said from behind her. "Well, I don't think anyone needs to see this, do they?" He turned and shut the door.

Oh my God. She swallowed her mouthful, mortified that she had forgotten he was there for a moment. She met his eyes, shame flushing her cheeks. He cracked his neck, laced his fingers together, and popped them as he stretched. What…?

He rolled up his sleeves and stood next to her. "You probably think you're all that, but frankly, you're a rank amateur. Watch and learn, grasshopper."

In, like, two seconds he had two sandwiches in his mouth, and was double fisting one hand of chips, and one of grapes. He was…freaking awesome. She eyed him and grabbed some more bread. He gave her a deadpan look as she met his eyes.

Okay then. She smeared the bread on a stick of butter and ate it, slowing down marginally.

He raised his eyebrows at her as he grabbed a banana. He bit off the end and started peeling it with his teeth, since his other hand still had some kind of cold cuts in it. She paused to watch in fascination as she finished her own mouthful and then grabbed a banana, too.

She'd taken two bites before he seemed to choke.

"Oh no. It doesn't count if you throw it all up, you know," she said. "You totally lose points for that."

He swallowed, the back of his hand pressed to his mouth as if he was keeping the food well and truly inside. He cleared his throat. "Put that banana down. That was cheating."

She paused and looked at it in her hand. *What? Ohhhhh.* She flushed, then giggled. She opened her mouth, eyes wide, as if she was going to eat the whole thing in one bite and then, as his eyes flickered down to her mouth, she threw it back on her plate. She immediately grabbed another hunk of bread and whispered "sucker" as she got a head start on him. It took him a good two seconds before he stopped staring and started chomping on his cold cuts. She grinned at him as best she could while her mouth overflowed with the warm bread.

She was no longer afraid that someone would stop her eating. Out of the corner of her eye, she saw him palm a chicken wing. She hadn't seen them, so she slid around his back to reach that side of the table. She managed one before the sheer amount of food started swelling her belly.

"Urgh. I can't…" She stepped back from the table. What had she done? Her stomach started rolling inside. Oh no. There was no way she was going to waste the food she'd eaten.

"Go sit down." Will nodded at the sofa against the far wall. "See? I knew you were punching above your weight, sweetheart. Not counting the banana, of course."

She smiled inside, but her mouth wouldn't let her make the actual movement. She sat gingerly on the sofa and slowly leaned back, hoping her stomach would appreciate the stillness. One deep breath. Two. Okay. That was better. Ahhhh.

Anya closed her eyes as a sleepiness invaded her body. She knew she shouldn't relax, but the rest of her was too tired and full to care. The sofa shifted under her as Will sat down a respectable distance from her.

"How d'you feel?" he asked in a low voice.

"Like the Hulk is sitting on my belly and singing me a lullaby," Anya whispered back, eyes still closed. His proximity was making her more awake, though, and she wondered if she had the energy to get up again. He smelled so good up close. All clean and soapy. Like when she sat in the laundromat, and when no one was looking buried her face in her warm clothes. Clean and comforting.

He snorted a laugh in reply. "So how is this going to work?" he asked after a long moment.

"What? How does what work?" she asked, eyes popping open and wondering where the conversation was headed.

"The interview thing. Are you going to write one big article, or smaller ones, or…just what are you planning?"

Good question. "I'm not 100 percent sure. I mean, this was kind of a last minute fill-in for a regular writer whose kid got sick. Well, to be honest, I'm more of a fill-in for a fill-in, since the other two available writers had kids on summer break and couldn't take two weeks off. I only heard yesterday that I'd be doing this."

"So you don't have any kids home for the summer?" he asked with an audible smile.

"I'm only…" Shit, how old was she? She'd allowed the magazine to assume she'd been in her twenties, told Natasha she was nineteen, but it sounded like LJ insisted everyone was in their late twenties. "I'm too young to have children," she settled on.

"So is everything we say on the record?" he asked.

She hauled herself upright and looked at him. "I guess? Unless you tell me it's not?" God, she wished she sounded more confident. "My plan is to write nightly blog posts for

WowSounds and maybe ask the readers for questions for you. Would that be okay?"

"Sure. Will I get to see what you write before you send it in?" He sounded anxious and that made her feel a whole lot more confident.

"I don't think so. Especially since I plan on blowing the lid off your deepest secret."

• • •

Holy mother of shit. He sprung up.

"What secret?" he demanded.

How could she possibly know?

And then, in that second, he took in her puzzled face and realized she meant that she was going to *look for* his deepest secret. Not that that was any better.

She folded her arms. "Just how many secrets do you have?"

Shit. Now who was the amateur?

"Oh. Okay." He searched his pathetic brain for an excuse. "I thought you'd figured out that I'm a competitive eater and was going to tell the world what I looked like with food hanging out of my mouth." He sat back down and kept on deflecting, deflecting, deflecting.

He laid his arm across the back of the sofa and turned in toward her. 'What's this?" He skimmed his finger down her cheek and swiped off a smudge. He leaned in and licked his finger, keeping his eyes on hers, remembering that Trevin had told him to charm Anya. "Hmmm, nice. Guacamole. I didn't even see it on the buffet." He pretended to tip his hat to her. She smiled at him, at first tentatively, and then full on.

It pretty much knocked his socks off. His heart raced, and he wondered if he dared kiss her.

I have no business wanting her this bad.

But he did want her. So much that it felt like he was going to explode if he didn't get to touch her.

Blood started pounding in his head with the realization that he was alone with her. He leaned in just the tiniest bit—

And then remembered that she could be conning him, too. She was a freaking reporter.

Blinking, he looked at the buffet and said, "You want to go for a second round, or do you want to take a walk?"

She was silent for a moment, and then she said, "Walk."

He jumped up. "You're such a lightweight." He grinned and helped her up. She took it, and the warmth of her hand in his took his mind right back to wanting to kiss her. He was turning into a fucking girl, for God's sake.

She dropped his hand, and they made their way outside.

"So there seems to be some friction between the members of the band," she said matter-of-factly.

He glanced at her, but her eyes were roving around the backstage area. "You sit on a bus with four other people for weeks on end and tell me if you ever snipe at someone. It's just bickering. We all get on fine."

"Really? Fine?" she asked mildly.

"Actually, all the guys...well, they seem to be settling down. One by one, they bit the dust."

"What do you mean 'bit the dust'?"

"Found true love. Or something like it, anyway." He looked at her again, wondering what she was thinking, and then realized what he'd said. "But you totally can't put that in your article. It's off the record. People know, obviously, but we try to keep it totally low-key when we're out and about, and having photos taken, or giving interviews. LJ doesn't want fans being turned off by the fact that some of the guys have girlfriends."

"Doesn't that mean the boys can have their cake and eat it, too? I mean, if they have secret girlfriends?"

"Eh. That's not really what happens. Firstly, they seem pretty content for the first time since I've known them" — virtually no time at all — "and secondly, it kind of protects the girls, too. We dispose of the hate mail directed at them. Some of it's pretty nasty."

"From fans?" she said with her adorable, inscrutable face.

"Only the psycho fans do that. Again, that's off the record. We don't officially call those fans psycho. We call them…what were the words that LJ used? Oh yes, 'committed fans.'"

"Should be committed you mean?" A smile played around her lips.

"Exactly. Sometimes, I'm not going to lie, they're scary. Like this is every guy's dream, right? Having virtually every girl want them. Scream for them. But the funny thing is, the more it happens, the more you want to get away. The more you want no one. The more you cling to those in the same situation. I think that's what happened. They bonded together, and eventually ended up getting sick of one another. So the bickering."

"That's…interesting." She stopped walking and removed her sunglasses. "Are we on the record?"

"Which bit?" His heart started beating faster as his mind filtered through the stuff he'd said. No, he couldn't think of anything controversial…

"You said 'they.' 'They' banded together. And 'you think' that's what happened. If they are 'they' what are you? And why don't you know what's been happening?"

Shit shit shit shit.

"Off the record," was all he could think of to say.

She remained silent as she looked at him.

"Come on, Lois Lane." That should take her mind off his slip.

• • •

WowSounds.com
Tulsa welcomes Seconds to Juliet!
By your reporter-on-the-ground, Anya Anderson

Who has two thumbs and saw S2J rehearse their show's final number today? This girl. When I got the email asking me to cover for the person who was covering for the person who couldn't take two weeks in the summer to follow S2J, I confess, I felt like I had a lot of research to do.

But now that I'm here, immersed in rehearsals, security, screaming fans, and, yes, Will Fray, I wonder if not being prepared, and not having assumptions based on previous interviews, is really the better way to play this gig.

Maybe I'll bring you information that you never thought about before, like…oh, let's say, who I saw almost come to blows this afternoon, or how amazing that show finale is…and maybe you'll stick around to help educate me.

So riddle me this: who is Will Fray? Well, this is your opportunity to tell me everything you think I should know about him and to ask any question you have for him. Each night I'll pick one question from the commenters to pose to the shyest member of S2J. How d'ya like them apples, S2J fans?

Chapter Five

Matt woke early. He didn't know what the others had been doing the night before, probably a poker game with the roadies, but they had rocked the bus when they came to bed at around three a.m. He figured from past form that they would probably get up just in time to grab coffee and turn up at the morning meeting. Which gave him at least an hour to put the coffee on, have a shower, and do a little Google search on his new shadow before they all got up.

It wasn't that he didn't like them, he just tried to avoid too much interaction with them, because the closer he got to them, the more they might suspect something wasn't quite right about Will. He had next-to-no idea what his brother had told them about his life, so he had no way to reiterate what he'd already said. So there were no bonding chats, or having a beer and confessional, which the others did often.

From his bunk, he'd heard about who had the secret hookups with fans, who was on anxiety meds his mom had slipped him that had been flushed dramatically by Ryder, who'd claimed he needed to feel the fear and stop being a pussy. He'd learned how Miles had lost his virginity, and that one of them hadn't yet. When he'd listened to that particular conversation, he'd been sure that they would take the piss and call him out every chance they got. But they didn't. They'd all been surprisingly gentle.

That night from his bunk, he'd wondered if he could come clean about Will and if they'd be that supportive of him, too. He never took that chance, though. Will and his mom were the most important people in his life, and he wasn't hanging them out to dry on the off chance that someone wouldn't spill the beans. Will might have loved these guys, but he barely knew them. And he guessed there was a reason Will'd only told Trevin about the swap.

After putting the coffee on, he booted up his laptop and sneaked his glasses from his bunk. His twin didn't wear glasses, and so far, Matt had gotten away with contacts. But first thing in the morning, well, he just didn't like poking at his eyes that early in the day.

The letter that authorized his shadow revealed her name as Anya Anderson. Must remember that. He put the name into Google and sat back.

Fifty thousand hits. All right, then…

He stretched, cracked his knuckles, and clicked on the first WowSounds link: Tulsa welcomes Seconds to Juliet. It was a blog post, short, and kind of funny. She wrote well. There were already tons of comments and he scrolled through them idly before reaching the bottom of the page where there was a link saying "More articles from Anya Anderson." He clicked.

Two came up: "Where the people on the streets have no name." and "Alone at last?" Wow. She'd written a really long article last month about the homeless situation in Tulsa and a slightly shorter one about being lonely versus being alone. The longer one was about how politicians tried not to use the word "homeless," which left the people on the street called transients, or just unspoken of.

He relaxed back into the booth and looked out of the window onto the parking lot. So this was the kind of article she normally wrote. She must think the band to be a huge waste of time. Oh my God. She must have thought the excess food thing last night obscene. Last night...

His mind flashed back to the darkened room, the food, and wanting so much to kiss her. He pressed down on his pants to stop anything unfortunate happ—

"Bit early to be looking at porn, isn't it, dude?" Ryder said, coming from the bunk area, scratching his hair with both hands.

Instant shrinkage.

"So funny. Coffee?" Matt nodded toward the machine, snatching off his glasses and stuffing them in his pajama pants pocket.

Ryder grunted and stretched, showing all his tattoos under his wife-beater. The others were stirring in the back, so Matt quickly read the rest of the article but didn't have time to read the "Alone at last?" one. He bookmarked it and looked for any other mentions of her. There weren't any. In fact, this Anya Anderson didn't appear to be anywhere else. No Facebook, no Instagram, no Tumblr. Weird.

He closed the laptop and waited for the onslaught of band members. Luckily it was show day, so no one would shower until later. Jockeying for position in the shower usually brought the worst arguments of the day, so show days were a relief. They showered twice on show days—before makeup and then after the performance. The latter was a much shorter event since they often came offstage soaking wet from the last number.

It was already 9:40 a.m., so there wasn't much time before the mandatory 10:00 a.m. meeting. Matt slipped out of the booth with his laptop and went back to his bunk. Grabbing a hoodie, he closed the curtain on his personal space and headed back out to the living area of the bus. He topped off his coffee and left, planning to sit on the steps and drink until they were all ready for the meeting.

His place was already taken. Anya.

From behind, he noticed her hair was damp from the shower, and her T-shirt was creased so badly he couldn't see what was written on the back. "Morning," he said.

"Morning." She closed her notebook and stuck her pen down its spiral spine.

He took a sip of coffee and tried to ignore the sweet smell coming from her skin, or maybe her hair. Something edible. Vanilla, maybe. He wanted nothing more than to lean in and see exactly where it was coming from. To lick her neck or something.

God. I am such a perv.

And then he realized that he definitely didn't smell as fresh and as lovely as she did, and he shuffled away a little on the step. She looked at him and frowned.

"It's…uh, you smell so good and I realized I probably didn't…you see it's show day and we don't shower… I mean, we shower. Of course we shower. At least twice. But later."

Kill me now.

She just smiled, which amplified his discomfort by a factor of about fifty. He needed to kiss her or something to get it out of his system. Yeah, right. That only happened in movies. She'd probably slap him.

"So what are we doing today?" she asked, staring out over the parking lot and the now empty barriers. He followed her eyes. A handmade poster was still tied to the metal fence. It said, "Will Fray, have my baby."

"Yeah." He ducked his head and tried to channel Will's more introverted side.

"Is that how it's usually done? Propositioning you guys via posters? What do you think when girls do that?"

He grinned, unable to help himself from answering. "Well, I always carefully consider every offer, of course, but this one's persistent. She keeps asking me, but I don't know, man, I'm not sure I'd look good with swollen ankles, you know?"

He didn't envy his brother having to deal with this, especially as shy as he really was. Ironically, despite Will having a much better voice than his brother, Matt was more outgoing, so could probably handle the intensity of the fan attention better, yet Matt was too scared of being found out to be able to enjoy any of the adulation.

"Probably not a good look for you," Anya agreed solemnly. "Are we still going to the homeless shelter?"

Yes, yes, yes. This was a perfect way to impress her. "I think so. We'll find out more at the morning meeting. We think it's important to highlight local issues in the towns where we perform. It might not do anything, but at least it brings the media to these places, don't you think?" He knew how pathetically eager for approval he sounded.

"I'm sure they appreciate it," she replied mildly.

It was almost as if she hadn't just written a long article on the local homeless population. "I read your article this morning. It was very well written. You must have spent ages with those people to have them open up to you like that."

She didn't reply.

"Your blog post last night has already got hundreds of comments, you know," he said.

That got her attention. "Really?" She seemed surprised.

"You didn't check this morning?" he asked. Even the band looked up their reviews the morning after the show. Seasoned professionals didn't, but they still valued the feedback, even though it could sometimes mess with your head.

"It didn't occur to me." She frowned. "How many did you say?"

"I don't know…hundreds."

She didn't look happy. Not in the slightest.

• • •

I'm not happy.

Hundreds? Her heart beat faster at the thought of people at WowSounds actually noticing her. Flying under the radar was her modus operandi. It worked for being on the street, loitering in libraries, sitting with one cup of tea for hours in a café. She didn't want to get too much attention for doing this job. Enough to get a decent check. Not enough that people paid attention to her.

Was a hundred comments good? Was it too many? Not enough? Would people notice that there were too few comments?

When she got back, she'd have to look at them. Figure out if it was good or bad. Find the next question to ask, that is, if everyone didn't already know everything about him.

So she had that to worry about now, in addition to the visit to the homeless shelter. What if someone saw her? Recognized her as being homeless herself? She pressed her hand to her chest as if to still the rise of anxiety.

Sure, she could spin some story about how she was actually a reporter and had been "pretending" to be homeless, but she was already knee-deep in deception as it was. If she had to spin even more lies on top of that, she might drown. Added to which, people in the shelter had trusted her with their stories, related to her as a fellow homeless person. There was no way she could betray them by pretending to be something she wasn't. And they *would* feel betrayed.

"Do you want to come to our morning meeting? They only last about ten minutes. LJ just goes through the day's activities, which will be this one excursion and the show. You're coming to the show, right?"

Was she? "I don't know. Do I need a ticket?" Because she had fourteen dollars to her name and she was sure that a concert ticket would cost more than that.

"No, you'll be backstage. You can watch from the wing if you like." He shrugged like he didn't really care about the answer, but his eyes searched for hers. She recognized the look as one she saw a lot on the streets and wondered why a pop star would be so insecure. Or maybe it was just about his performance onstage. Or maybe he *was* the Shy Guy everyone called him.

"I'd like to watch, if I won't be in the way," she said.

"Nah." He floated a hand over the small of her back to direct her back toward the stage. "There's a platform above the stage on each side so you can see us, but we won't run into you when we're trying to do a costume change. No cell phones are allowed backstage, though."

Not a problem, since she didn't have a phone anyway. "Okay." Her stomach was churning worse than it ever had on the street. She was a fraud, and she wasn't used to the constant nagging feeling from lying about who she was. It was giving her a new kind of stomachache.

They arrived at the meeting, held in the front row of the arena. "Um, would you, um, do you think you'd want to ask me any questions while we're alone here?" he asked.

He was so weird when he was hesitant and shy. But he was right, she should be better at this. Maybe if she concentrated on him, rather than how she was feeling, she'd do a better job. A professional job.

"Sure, why not?" She scrambled for her notebook. "Umm. Hang on."

He laughed quietly at her.

"What? What's so funny?" she said, flipping over the pages, trying to find the place where she'd written some initial questions. Hell, why couldn't she remember them?

"Nothing. I just figured you'd have like twenty questions off the top of your head that you'd want answers to. Maybe even questions I'd never been asked before."

She stopped her flicking. "You want me to ask you questions that you probably haven't been asked before? Okay. What's your second favorite breakfast food?"

A blank expression came over his face and she took a turn to laugh at him. "Come on, Will. These are the things that readers of WowSounds want to know." She shrugged and licked the tip of her pen as if she was ready to write down every single word he said. Nodding encouragingly, she said, "Come on…it's an easy question."

"Second favorite breakfast food? Okay, if you insist. It's fried bread." He crossed his arms and sat back in the stadium seat.

"Fried what?"

"Fried bread."

"I'm not sure…is that even a breakfast food?" She wasn't sure it was food at all. It sounded totally gross.

He threw an arm out melodramatically, a million miles from the stuttering boy he'd been a few minutes earlier. "Imagine, if you will, a perfectly cooked breakfast. Sizzling bacon, fried eggs… But what's that I hear you say? We need some carbs? And we don't have any biscuits? Well then. Take a slice of totally ordinary Wonder Bread and chuck it in the fat the bacon and eggs have just cooked in. Fry it until it's all nice and crispy and serve with the egg on top."

"I thought you were a vegetarian. Or was that one of the other guys?" Gah, she wished she'd known that she was only going to be able to interview Will. She'd wasted a bunch of time scanning fan sites and she'd forgotten who was who.

He went white and his lower lip went all stiff. Oh, maybe he *was* the vegetarian. Why was he so scared? Maybe he had some kind of a marketing deal with a vegetarian company? "Don't worry, even vegetarians get a pass on bacon. I mean, how can you not? Ah-ha!" She'd found the questions she'd listed. "Found them."

"What?" He still seemed shocked, and she couldn't fig-ure out why. Was she really putting on such an amateur show that he was stunned she found her questions? She needed to get her game on—the last thing she needed was for Will to complain about her to LJ. She had to stay.

She cleared her throat. "How do you like being on tour? Do you get homesick?" There. That sounded like a question a trained reporter might ask.

Color came back to his cheeks as his face relaxed into a normal expression. Mentally she fist pumped. Nailed it. Now she sounded professional.

"We love touring. We love seeing our fans and putting on the best show we possibly can. I do miss my mom, though," he said.

Luckily, she could write fast. But shit, now she needed a follow-up question. "Um. What do you miss most about your home? No. You already told me that. Okay, describe your bedroom to your fans."

He laughed out loud at the question. "You're getting very intimate now. I think I'm not going to answer that one. If I found a special fan…maybe, just maybe I'd let her see my bedroom herself."

"And has there *been* a special fan who's seen your room?" She was rocking the reporter-chat now.

He sat up straight and looked past her with a blank expression. Then he sighed heavily, a little dramatically. "I haven't found that special girl yet. But I keep on looking. At every tour stop, I keep on looking."

"Nice answer. I bet you have embarrassing posters on the wall, don't you?"

"If I did, and that's a big 'if,' they would definitely have disappeared by the time anyone saw them, I can tell you that!"

Before she could reply, the rest of the band appeared in a loud group. Anya looked down at her notebook and tried to relax, but boisterous people set her nerves on edge, and she fought an instinct to slink away. An instinct that had kept her safe on the streets. Jude had taught her that. A homeless war veteran, Jude had found her during her first month on the street and had given her plenty of advice. Loud men indicated either alcohol, or a euphoria/adrenaline rush that lowered inhibitions. Where they may walk past her on a regular day, in this state—amped up guys together—they could mean trouble.

But not these guys. Not today.

She took a deep breath.

Chill out, girl. Chill. Out.

Someone grunted and dropped into a seat near her. She glanced over and saw…LJ. Not looking at her. But that didn't mean he wasn't watching her.

Okay, that thing about chilling out?

Not going to happen.

Chapter Six

She was weird. Fucking sexy, but weird. She was shaking in her chair like she was having a seizure, but she wasn't. She was doodling in her book. So weird. He wondered if she knew she looked like a child hiding. She was a freaking hop, skip, and a jump away from curling up in a ball and rocking back and forth.

Huh. She'd seemed comfortable enough yesterday. What had changed since then?

His eyes found LJ's again. The manager had been staring at Matt while he was answering Anya's questions, just waiting for him to say the wrong thing, he just knew it. That's why he'd gone off on the "special girl" bullshit. It was "on message," approved by their PR team. He couldn't pull him up on anything. But then LJ started to eye Anya, and before he knew it, Matt was out of his seat and had plonked down in the one on the other side of Anya, putting himself between Anya and LJ.

Don't fuck with her, too, you bastard.

She was probably bat-shit psychotic, but she was *his* bat-shit psychotic.

Before he had a chance to question his own sanity for caring about what happened to the weirdo he had to charm, the PR lady started to speak. She read them in on the homeless shelter, which made Anya stop shaking. Small miracles. But after reading her article about life on the streets, he was pretty happy that today was the homeless shelter. Maybe she would be more likely to warm to him.

After the meeting, they were left alone in the stadium, as Anya didn't make a move after everyone else had left. So he just sat beside her, waiting for her to finish her doodle. It looked like a man...maybe. He craned. Could be a chicken. Drawing probably wasn't one of her talents. But as he watched the picture take shape, he saw it was a man, bundled up in a hooded coat, with a rucksack on his back. Okay, so she was no Monet, but it wasn't bad. At least he could tell what it was now.

"Who's that?" he asked as she applied the last few lines of shading on the ground beneath him.

She jumped, like whoa. He held his hands up in a gesture of 'Hey, I'm not armed' and said, "Don't worry, it's okay, calm down."

She looked around and seemed startled that they were all alone. "Sorry. I... When did everyone leave?"

"About five minutes ago. It's okay, I'd rather be here than playing World of Warcraft in the bus, which is all we do between interviews and visits.

"Wow. I'm sorry. I must have really..." She looked back at her drawing and bit her lip.

Sweet Jesus, he wanted to wrap his arms around her and hug away whatever was wrong with her. "Who is he? Did you meet him when you wrote your article about the homeless?" He could see now that that's exactly what he was: a homeless man.

She hesitated and ran her fingers over the pencil drawing, smudging it a little. "Yes. His name is Jude and he introduced me around, and then when I tried to find him again, I couldn't. I keep looking, every time I'm in downtown Tulsa, but I haven't seen him. I hope he's okay."

"Hey, maybe he'll be at the homeless shelter we're going to this afternoon." he said.

"He never really liked them. I might ask when I'm there, though," she said.

Silence descended. He had to do something to break the downer mood. He looked at the seats around him. "Do you know who comes to our shows?"

"Girls? Lots and lots of girls, I guess?" she replied, with a furrowed brow.

"Hang on a sec." He raced to the sound platform in the middle of the arena and asked Jerry if he could find a file of "Not Tonight," one of their up-tempo tracks that he could put on speaker.

When he got back to her, she was already standing and watching him.

"So when you're onstage, a lot of times all you can see is the first ten rows or so of people, until they light up the whole audience at the end. So, whoever's in the front rows really set the mood of the show." The music came on. Loud, but not as loud as the rehearsal music had been.

"Let me show you how it goes. Come on." He grabbed

her hand and led her into the middle of the front row. "Some nights this is how it looks." He sat in one of the seats, leaned back and crossed his arms. "So who am I?"

"Me?" she said with a giggle. "That's probably how I'll be sitting."

Score. She was slipping out of her funk.

He assumed an outraged look on his face. "What? No way, sister. You're going to be slamming some moves. I want to see you dancing whenever I look at you. If you don't, you'll get a dare at the end of every show. No. I'm a mid-level industry professional. I've been given tickets, and I'm here just so I can tell people I had front row seats at the Seconds to Juliet concert to show how important I am."

"Wow. That happens?" she asked.

"More than we'd like, yeah. One day, I swear I'm going to stop singing and tell them they have to get up and dance. I'd probably be fired, but man, it would be worth it."

She laughed, the sound penetrating the music and sending a warm feeling through him.

"Okay, who am I now?" He waited a beat and then started dancing, deliberately awkward and off the beat.

"Oh my God, like parents trying to be cool."

"I don't think you really believe that. Maybe you have to feel it. Come on. Dance with me." She backed away a couple of steps but he caught her hand. He drew her in close and swayed her against him. Hell, she felt good. Her vanilla scent definitely came from her hair and he was in a perfect position to take a good whiff. He bit back a groan and spun her out. She rotated nicely under his arm, and then he made her dance like him.

"Like this?" she asked between laughs. She popped her

arms out on the downbeat, and matched that with weird kicks.

"You're a natural."

"We are someone's unfortunate parents, aren't we?" she panted.

He stopped dancing and admitted, "We could be. But I was thinking more of LJ. Watch him tonight for a real treat.

"And now? He pressed himself to the barrier and screamed, "Ry-der! Ry-der! Ry-der I love you!" all through the music.

"Crazed fan who wants to get in Ryder's pants?" she said.

"Maybe that one was too easy. How about this?"

He grabbed her and pulled her to him. Oh yeah, he was bad. He held her carefully with one hand in hers and one pressed against her lower back. He swung her around in time to the music. "Okay, I'm not actually going to do this, but imagine I'm totally grinding myself against you. Like we're virtually having sex right here."

"That's kind of gross," she said, smiling.

"Imagine trying to sing a song and just not being able to take your eyes off them. Yeah, some guys totally use us to score with the girls. More power to them, I guess. But I won't lie, sometimes I feel like we need to have a hose onstage for people like that."

The music faded to silence.

"It must be pretty distracting to see that while you're trying to perform," she said, oddly quiet despite the silence of the stadium.

He looked down into her eyes and hesitated. "I think I might have a new distraction tonight." Where the hell had that come from?

Her cheeks flushed red and her eyes dropped to his chest and then up again. She took a step back and wagged her finger at him. "Don't think you can sweet-talk me into going easy on you."

"Busted!" he replied. Except…no. It was better for her to think that it'd been a joke. Better. Safer. More honorable? Crap. She was messing with his head. Was she doing it deliberately? Was this shy-girl persona just a routine to reel in the shy guy?

Come on, Matt. You need to keep your wits about you. Stop sabotaging yourself. Keep her at arm's length.

He lightly punched her shoulder, like he would a sister. "You caught me. But I'm serious. Watch LJ tonight. You won't regret it. It's a dance for the ages. Come on, let's go get in the van. You're about to witness the insanity of us getting off the compound!"

· · ·

Insanity was right.

As the bus wove through the congested city roads, honking car horns and people banging on the sides of the bus punctuated their trip. Each time a bunch of girls screamed and threw themselves against the doors, Anya jumped out of her skin. It was like the Hemsworth brothers were in town. Or…well, there wasn't really anything else to compare it with.

It seemed to her as if the guys in the band barely noticed the commotion they were causing. Mostly their heads were down, eyes on their phones or iPads.

She should spend her time writing in her notebook

about Will. Nothing earth shattering, just the details she could use in her long article.

Off the record girlfriends?

Psycho Fans.

"They banded together…" Distant from the others?

Fried Bread.

Vegetarian?

Will sat across the aisle from her with earphones on, so when she was done writing she just watched them in their own little worlds. She wondered who was texting a girlfriend, and who was playing Candy Crush. Will was obviously immersed in music and she wondered what he listened to. Even though she strained to hear, she couldn't.

The brakes screamed to a halt in an area she knew well. St John's in the Vale shelter. It was run by a church, in fact it was attached to a red brick church. The priest knew her. Had always been concerned about her and she really hoped he wouldn't blow her cover. Her anxiety rose to the surface, creating a vacuum in her stomach that was as familiar to her as her hand. The street was totally stopped up with crowds of people, heaving like it was filled to the brim with shoppers on Black Friday.

Police had created a tiny path for the band to get into the shelter.

"Are you ready?" Will asked her, taking off his headphones.

"This is crazy." Kneeling on the seat, she peered out of the window. "I…it's scary out there."

"No kidding. Just smile as if it's the most natural thing in the world." He took his place in line at the front of the bus.

The tour director said, "Boys first. Extras will be disembarked a minute after they get inside the building." Anya sat back down again since she and one other woman seemed to be the only "extras." The screaming rose to fever pitch outside as the boys descended the steps. The band was instantly rendered invisible by the crowd.

Her gaze fell on Will's headphones. While taking a quick look around the bus, she grabbed the headphones and pressed play on his iPod. Holding them to one ear, she instantly recognized the song Will had just made her dance to in the stadium. He was still listening to the band's own music. That was…borderline…strange? She filed that nugget of information and made a mental note to ask him what other bands he listened to.

"Extras. Follow me," the tour director said over the hiss of the automatic door.

Anya followed her. The crowd was less frenzied, but she was stunned when people started to aim their cell phones at her. She ducked her head. The last thing she needed was her mom or anyone recognizing her. Oh hell, even anyone at WowSounds. That would be really bad.

Not that she'd lied to them, but she certainly hadn't disabused them of the notion that she was in her twenties. Like, far in her twenties. And that she'd written for other publications.

And the crowd was still deafening. It took every inch of self-control not to curl up into a ball under the van. Or to run and hide—anywhere away from the heaving masses. But she stood and, as if her insides weren't rioting, walked down the corridor the police had made for them.

Inside, the familiar setup of tables and cots brought back memories. Anyone was allowed to stay there for three nights in a row, but after that, Father Howard felt duty bound to call social services. He called it a three day sanctuary. After that, all bets were off. He said he answered to God and his conscience. She hadn't been there at all since the previous winter. When it was warm enough she tried to stay on the street. It was actually easier to blend in with the drunk college students and fly under the police's radar.

Will nodded her over. "If you write about this, will you mention this place by name please? Any publicity it can get, the more donations they'll receive. You can say I personally asked fans to donate clothes, food, and supplies. That should keep them stocked until the new year."

Yeah right. "The new year? That's six months away. Do you know how many people come through here each week? How many meals they have to cook?"

He frowned. "I do, actually. The priest just told me. We toured a place like this in Atlanta, asked for donations, and they had to find somewhere to store all the things that turned up. Their shelter was twice the size of this one, and they had to re-donate the items to other shelters."

"Oh. I…" She suddenly felt embarrassed for assuming to know more than he did about it. "I didn't realize…"

"It's okay. I had no idea what we could achieve until we started on this tour. Our fans are amazing. I know we dig at them, and call some of them psychos, but the vast majority of the ones who don't scare the pants off us are awesome."

She looked around and saw the rest of the band members sitting on cots and at tables chatting to the people who were staying there. Tears threatened to bubble out of her eyes. She sniffed and looked away. How many young guys would do this? Would care enough to do more than send a check? How many would actually sit with people like her and talk to them about their lives? Hell. She'd kind of assumed they were all flash and no substance.

"Are you going to cry?" Will asked, grinning.

"No. What? No way." Anya opened her eyes wide to try to dry the film of water just hovering there.

"Awww, you're so cute. Don't worry. We're complete dicks, too. Does that help?" His arm slipped around her shoulders, and she shrugged it off.

"Too right you're a dick. I'm not crying." She turned away and saw Father Howard looking directly at her over his half-rim glasses. He nodded to indicate his office, and she gave a small nod back. "I'll be right back."

"Okay, I'll be here trying to think of ways to show you what a dick I am." He grinned.

"Don't worry on my account. You're already doing a great job," she replied as she turned away.

Father Howard was in his office, sitting behind his small desk and peering at his old computer. As she walked in, he motioned to her to close the door. She did.

"Anya. It's a pleasure to see you. Do I have to be worried about you arriving with this boy band?" He shifted back into his chair and crossed his arms over his cassock.

Her brow furrowed. "What do you mean, worried?"

"I mean, the last time I saw you, you were living down by the river. And you know I don't mean in those penthouse apartments. And now you're arriving with boys who are in town for only a few days. I'm asking if you're all right."

"Oh. *Oh*. No, nothing like that. You know the article I wrote for that online magazine last month? They asked me to cover the band on this leg of their tour. That's all." She sat in a small armchair under an even smaller window.

"They asked a sixteen-year-old to follow a band and write an article?" His expression clearly said he didn't believe her.

"Not...exactly. Firstly, I had a birthday last month. I'm seventeen now. And while they might think I'm older, I never actually *told* them I was older. I've never met anyone who works at the magazine, I've only dealt with them over email. I just...thought it would maybe help me get"—she sniffed—"back on my feet?"

"Oh. Okay, fair enough. Keep your head down, Anya. We don't want your mother finding you again."

She blew air out of her cheeks as she thought about what he said. Her mother wouldn't ever try to find her again. But she'd never told Father Howard that, in case he thought their non-existent relationship was Anya's fault. In some way it had to be, because why else would her mom have left her in the middle of the night without arranging for care or anything? But she hadn't wanted him thinking badly of her, thinking she'd done something wrong. "I don't want that. She's probably left town. Probably back in California by now."

"Let's hope. Listen. There's nothing, and I mean nothing, I want to see more than you making a success of your life. You're due, you know? So be careful of those boys. They're here, and God knows I appreciate that. But they are still teenage boys." He gave her a stern look, although he couldn't stop his eyes from twinkling.

"Yes, Father," she said, trying not to smile.

"Okay. Good then." He made a slightly sloppy sign of the cross in her direction and said, "May God grant you his favor in your endeavors."

"Amen," she replied as obediently as she had been taught at her Catholic school, before they'd turned her in to child services.

"I'm going to be reading your tour article, young lady," he warned.

"Father. Can I ask? Have you seen Jude around at all?" Her voice cracked on the last work.

"Oh Anya." He removed his glasses and placed them carefully on the table in front of him as if he was wondering what to say. "I haven't seen him since last November. I'm hoping the VA is looking after him at last."

Her heart took a dive. "I don't think they are. I think if he was better, or safe, he would have come looking for me. I keep going back to his spot under the bridge, but he hasn't been there, and no one's seen him."

"Well don't worry about Jude. He wouldn't want you to be concerned about him, would he? Now go out there and write a great article about this shelter " His eyes twinkled as he put his glasses back on.

"Yes, Father. Thank you," she said jumping up. "I'd better go before I miss my ride."

He just nodded and went back to his computer. He still looked at it like it was likely to bite him at any moment. Some things never changed.

When she got back into the shelter, only Will was left. "What happened? What did I miss?"

"The bus, for one thing." He didn't look too happy about it.

"They left without us? Without you?" she asked.

He rolled his eyes. "It's Miles's party trick. Once he gets on the bus, he tells the guys onboard that one of us is asleep in the back, or in the john or something, and she's usually so distracted that she just tells the driver to leave."

"What do we do now?"

He produced a pair of scratched sunglasses and what can only be described as a flowerpot rain hat with "The Bruins" on the front. "This is my disguise. The lady in the kitchen gave them to me."

"It's a good one. No one is going to come near us with you looking like that," Anya said, biting back a smile.

"We're leaving through the back. If the navigation on my phone is correct, it looks easy enough to just walk. It'll take a while, but I don't get much freedom to walk around anymore."

"Sure." She spent her whole life walking, so it didn't bother her at all. Maybe it would be a good time to ask some questions. "Sounds like fun."

"Let's hit the road." He held out his elbow in a gentle-manly gesture, and she slid her arm through it.

"After you. The big bad world awaits your presence," she said. "What could possibly go wrong with this?" Rolling her eyes at his fake frown, she continued. "You know, if anyone does recognize you, we might not get out alive." She looked him up and down. "Or at least clothed."

He hesitated for a minute as if he was contemplating having his clothes ripped off in downtown Tulsa. Hah! She'd rattled him. He bit his lip as he stared at the door they were about to go through.

"Nah. That's not going to happen. Anyway, if you're not living life on the edge, you're taking up too much room."

"I'm going to remind you that you said that."

Chapter Seven

Anya seemed really tense as they left the shelter. Her head swiveled constantly from side to side, and he wondered if she'd ever been to this part of town before. She seemed scared. He felt an irresistible urge to wrap his arm around her and protect her.

"Don't worry. I'm sure we'll be out of the neighborhood soon. I won't let anyone harass you." At his words, she frowned and her step faltered.

"I'm not scared. I've spent a lot of time here."

Urgh. I'm such an ass.

Of course she'd spent a lot of time here—she'd written that long piece about the homeless problem in Tulsa. "I'm sorry. I forgot that. It was a great article. It felt like you'd known those people for years."

She took her arm out of his. What had he said now?

Charm her, Matt. Dammit.

Weirdly, a slice of him really wanted her to like him.

Wanted to penetrate the puzzle, to have her eyes warm over as she looked at him. Jaysus. What the actual fuck? Could he be turning into his own freaking brother? All moonlight and effing roses? What was wrong with him?

"So are you from around here?" he asked, realizing he didn't really know anything about her beyond her extreme love of food.

"Not too far from here," she replied in a low voice.

He wondered how she could be so animated sometimes when talking about stupid things like dancing and propositions on posters, but so restrained when he asked her about herself. "Do you have a big family?"

If possible her voice got even smaller. "Not really." She raised her eyes to meet his. "It's really just been me since I left school."

He was overwhelmed with a weird sensation in his stomach. Was she really alone? Was he supposed to leave it there? Ask more? He opted for the latter. Surely no one got into trouble for taking too much interest in a girl. You know, unless stalkering.

"So no brothers or sisters?" Then he stopped. He didn't want her asking the same question of him. So he didn't give her a chance to answer. "Okay, forget that, what is *your* second favorite breakfast food?"

She smiled at last. "Leftover pizza. Cold if possible."

He faked a gag. "Bleugh. That's horrible. And unnatural. Pizza is made to burn the roof of your mouth. Cold it's just…" He searched for the right description. "…a damp towel with chilly, wet vegetables on it." He gave an exaggerated shiver.

She shook her head. "I'm sorry, Will." She stopped and held out her hand to shake his.

Instinctively he put his hand in hers, only to have her continue.

"We can no longer be friends. Your position on cold pizza is frankly nothing short of…" she paused, "…un-American. We will have to part ways here."

She shook his hand, and he snatched it away, laughing. "You can't leave me now, you don't have a story yet!" Oh God, why had he said that?

"That is also true. Okay, I'll stay. But only until I find out your deepest, darkest secrets. Deal?"

"Deal," he choked.

Silence fell briefly as he tried to think of something to say. It was a warm day and walking in the midday sun probably wasn't the best of ideas. In truth, he could have easily hailed a taxi, or called LJ-the-Devil, or just asked some obliging passerby for a ride. But he hadn't.

"Can I get some proper questions in while we're walking?" she asked, breaking the weird tension between them.

"Sure. You have me alone for about an hour right now; it would be a shame to miss the opportunity of stellar one-on-one time, right?"

"An hour you figure? I think it will be a lot less time. I have three dollars that you'll be mobbed by the time we get halfway back."

He was about to reply when he noticed that as she was walking, she was absently sticking her fingers into the cash return dishes of all the parking meters as she went along. "Is the three dollars you have in quarters?"

She looked at him and then at her hand. Snatching her hand away from the meter she was molesting, she shrugged.

"It's all money. I have dollar bills, too." She really looked offended. So weird.

"I'll take that bet. Anyway, do you have questions for me?" *Three dollars? Totally random.*

"Sure. Let's start with some easy ones. What are you afraid of the most?"

Easy one. His brother was on record all over the place as saying he hated needles. "Needles. I can't have them anywhere near me without passing out. My pediatrician hated me."

"Where do you think that phobia came from?" she asked.

"I have zero idea. I prefer to think of it as a totally normal reaction to a stabby thing."

"You faint when you see a knife?"

"No, but then knives have other uses, like cutting up a delicious steak. Needles are just stabby things."

"Fair enough. Who was your first girlfriend?"

"Easy peasy." He'd ripped the crap out of his brother for dating when he was eleven. "Alice Singleton, ninth grade. She was blonde and wore glasses." A pang of nostalgia twanged at his stomach as he remembered how innocent and happy they'd both been until Will had discovered that he could sing and got himself on that damned TV show.

"Would you date her if you saw her again? I mean, she must know you're famous now." Anya smiled.

"I don't think Alice would be impressed. She definitely wasn't impressed with me back then. She was definitely more into the athletic guys. And that was never me."

"If you weren't a jock at school, who were you?"

He thought about the hours Will spent in his room making up songs after Alice had left him for a football player. "I was the misunderstood poet." He grimaced. Could he sound any more pretentious?

Oh well. It'd be Will who looked stupid, not him. Hah. He could have had much more fun with this if Will was better. Under normal circumstances, Matt would stitch him up on these interviews with stuff that Will'd have to deal with when he got back. Maybe when he was a little better. Maybe then he could claim Will had started learning Japanese, or the clarinet or something. He grinned to himself. He should start making a list.

"A poet? Do you think the stuff you write now is poetry?"

"I don't write much stuff now. But no. My poetry is strictly personal."

"Who was your first serious girlfriend then?"

"I haven't found my first serious girlfriend. Yet." Time to create a diversion before she got too close a look at his answers. And—hell—because, like it or not, he really wanted to know more about her. "I have a question for you."

"I'm not sure that's how this is supposed to work. But okay."

"Are you coming with us on our next tour stop?"

"I guess so. I'm with you for two weeks. The next stop is New Orleans, isn't it?"

"Yeah. It's a crazy place, though, and we're staying in the buses again. No hotel would put us up exclusively, so we're all up close and personal at the arena. Not sure if you'd want to go through that again."

"My bus is pretty empty except for Natasha and her clothes. So, yeah, I guess it's actually pretty full. But I don't have much stuff, so I'm fine in my bunk. You have to have hotels close, just so you can stay in them?"

"Yeah. One time we stayed in a hotel, it got crazy. There were girls everywhere, jumping from balcony to balcony, stealing room service uniforms. Management was really un-prepared for the frenzy the show brought. A thirteen-year-old fell from one of the balconies and broke her leg. It was horrible." Will had called home obviously upset about it and almost crying. Only Matt knew that the sniffs on the end of the phone was Will trying not to cry. The whole thing had been too overwhelming for him. He had no idea how the others managed, or hadn't. "So ever since then, we try to stay behind security at the arena, or at secret hotels where we can prearrange to be the only guests."

She didn't say anything, and he figured that she was maybe mentally writing her next blog post. A hot wind blew up the street, rustling litter and pushing Anya's black hair out of its clips. He walked half a step back. Her hair looked long, but she always seemed to pin it up, and he wondered what it would feel like down. *Look* like down. Not feel.

He grabbed his phone and started scrolling through the alerts he had for the band news. The pictures from the shelter had already hit the news feeds. They needed to get back to the arena. It was only a few blocks away, so hopefully no one would make the connection between what he was wearing at the shelter and what he was wearing now, but damn him for putting on a one-of-a-kind T-shirt with a line drawing of a whale on it. It was pretty distinctive.

"Will Fray?" a voice yelled from a shop.

Oh shit.

• • •

So she'd made three bucks today already; she was rolling in the green. Will grabbed her hand and yanked her along the road. She had to run to keep up with him. What the hell?

She was about to complain at being manhandled but they'd only gone half a block before people were staring and pointing and yelling. Wow. It felt like a full-blown media storm.

By the time she looked at where they were going, people were running alongside them with their cell phones thrust out.

"Watch out!" she shouted at a man who wasn't looking where he was going. Too late, he ran right into a parking meter and rebounded, falling into the gutter. She pulled her hand from Will's and was about to help him up when she saw the size of the throng following them. "Sorry," she gasped and kept on running. Her heart pounded but, instead of feeling terrified, a little euphoria cloaked the fear. She took another look at the crowd and couldn't help but giggle. At least she thought she'd giggled. She hadn't really giggled in about five years. The crowd was so loud now that she couldn't hear anything above the screaming and shouting of his fans.

Finally they gained a few seconds on their pursuers. They rounded a corner and he dragged her into a storefront. It was a posh men's store. They must have changed neighborhoods fast, but she knew from experience that you only had to cross a road to be in a totally different environment in Tulsa.

The bell on the door clanged and a perfectly styled man in a three piece suit—wow, but he must have been hot—emerged from the back of the store. "Can I help…" he began. He did a double take at Will, and then in a second took in the people rushing past the window. Will ducked behind a rack of suits, and Anya followed.

She peeked out between tweedy jackets. People were streaming past the window. And then some stragglers stopped and looked around them. Panting, they started to peer into all the shop windows.

"Quickly, hide in here," the shop owner said. He pointed through a door. Will grabbed her hand and ran, still crouching, into the room and slammed the door shut.

Darkness. Complete and total darkness.

"So what was that about living life on the edge?" she whispered.

"Very funny," he replied in the dark.

"Where are we?" Anya whispered.

"In a menswear store, Tulsa, United States of America. Did you bang your head?" he whispered back.

She went to push him, but she pushed thin air. "Not what I meant. Where are you?"

"I'm right here. Where's the light switch?" he said, a smile in his voice.

She groped the wall, feeling suddenly claustrophobic. Suddenly too hot and like she couldn't breathe. Shit. Frantically she searched for a light, but the walls were completely bare.

Her breath started to come in pants. "I can't find it. I can't find the light." She cringed at the panic she heard in her own voice.

Outside in the store, the door rang again as someone came in.

"Shhhhh," Will said.

"I can't, I can't…" she said. An arm snaked around her

waist and a hand covered her mouth.

"Shhhhh."

She wriggled free of his hand and couldn't help her heavy breathing. She sounded like a total mouth breather. He pulled her close and stroked her back, as if she were a baby that needed soothing. For some reason that pissed her off and she jerked free. "I'm not a baby!"

He took his arms away from her and she was suddenly chilled and alone in the dark. A whimper escaped her, but then she felt his light fingers in her hair. She turned her head into the caress, suddenly needing his touch. To not feel alone. It was an alien feeling, and she explored it with her mind, like fingers snaking over a braille book. Her breathing steadied. And she stepped back as the door opened in the shop again, bell jangling through the door.

"I'm sorr—" she began before his hand slid over her mouth.

"Shhhh."

Muffled voices came from the store, the words "Will Fray," however, were clear and repetitive. She stilled and listened intently. How many people were out there? Were they going to ransack the place? Were they safe? She'd seen first-hand what a mob mentality looked like during the Occupy demonstrations. People seemed to get out of hand much faster when they were in a group.

"I guess you're going to have an interesting story to blog tonight," he whispered against her ear. The intimacy of it made her stomach flicker with…a strange excitement that she hadn't felt since the Christmas Eve before her mom had left. His face was so close to hers that she felt his light exhale against her cheek.

She could so easily turn her head and kiss him. His lips must be just there. Then she realized his arm was around her and pressed against the small of her back. All of her was against him. She should step away.

She should step back maybe. Maybe go to the other side of the room. Open the door maybe. Maybe… All the while reveling in the feel of him. She hadn't been this close to another human since Jude gave her a quick hug good-bye six months ago. It had been a shock to both of them as neither of them were comfortable with touching, and she'd laughed at the awkwardness of the hug, and he had given one of his rare brief smiles.

Meanwhile, she still hadn't moved away from Will, but as soon as she realized that she wanted to wrap one of her own arms around him, she did step back. Moved back into a space of sanity. Where she wouldn't feel so tempted to kiss this…stranger.

What was wrong with her? One good meal and a safe place to sleep for a night and she was getting all hot and bothered by a boy. How soft. And dangerous.

The door swung open and the perfectly dressed man appeared. He stepped back to allow them out, and they peered into the room. "Oh sorry. I should have put the light on for you."

Anya looked back into the room, now illuminated by daylight, and discovered they'd been in a very comfortable dressing room with two comfy armchairs. If he'd switched on the light, that weird, very intimate ten minutes would never have happened.

"I got rid of them. I have a back door, but you might need to call someone to come get you. There are a lot of people still roaming around trying to find you.

"No problem," Will said. "Thank you very much for hiding us. Can I send you anything to thank you?"

"Please don't take this the wrong way, but could you send me an autographed photo of the gay one? Miles is it? It'll make a perfect birthday present for a good friend of mine."

Miles was gay? Was this the scoop she'd been looking for? Suddenly she hoped not. She wasn't sure how she'd feel about outing a boy. Yeah she did. That wasn't going to happen.

"Of course. No problem. Do you have a card? Write your friend's name down and I'll make sure he personalizes one for you."

The man scribbled and flushed as he handed the card to Will. It was kind of cute.

The car came after a few minutes with a driver Will didn't seem to know, and he held the door for her to slip into the back.

"Miles is gay?" she asked. She could have sworn there was some recent article about a childhood sweetheart. Aimee — that was it.

Will snapped on his seat belt and gave her a wicked smile. "Nah. He's English. But it's a fine line, you know?"

A strange feeling bubbled in her chest and a loud laugh-snort erupted from her closed mouth and therefore her nose. Her hands flew to her face in horror. Was that how she sounded when she laughed? She hadn't laughed properly in so long, but she was sure it didn't sound as mortifying as that.

"Did you just snort?" he laughed. His was perfect, of course. No snort. No worry there was snot coming out of his nose. "Excellent. Just when this day could not get any more worthwhile, you snort." He settled back into his seat and watched the streets fly by. "I've got ammo with Miles and now with you. Yup, it's a good day."

She flashed out a fist to punch his arm, but he caught her hand even while he was looking out of the window. He held her fist in his large hand for a second before turning back to her. She wanted to jerk her hand away, but the warmth and the rapport they were suddenly sharing made her hesitate. Why? She had no earthly clue. She pulled it away.

"So does that…insanity happen to you all the time?" she asked, still needing stuff for her blog post. In her head she was trying to separate the nuggets of information she got that she could use in her blog, to the long-con stuff she could write for the long article. *Long-con.* She couldn't believe she'd used that phrase. Classic Jude.

She sat up with intent. That's right. Jude. She wasn't looking to get cozy with Will. She needed the scoop. The thing she could sell for enough money to help get off the streets, and if she could find him, get Jude the help he deserved. She gazed out of the window, angry at herself for spending time looking into Will's eyes instead of watching the streets for Jude.

Dammit. She needed to get her mind back in the game.

Get the dirt, Anya.

Chapter Eight

Matt wracked his brain trying to remember what it had been like when Will first appeared on that stupid show. "In the beginning it was okay. I mean, when we were on the show, a lot of people preferred the other acts, so the attention wasn't that big. But as the other acts were voted off, there was more and more pressure to be single and available, and visible… and open, I guess."

The car bumped over a pothole and he almost fell into her lap. *Super-cool, dude.*

"You're pressured to be single?" she asked, looking back at him for the first time since he'd held her fist.

Shit. Was anyone supposed to know that? He couldn't remember. "At first we were. I mean, I don't think anyone minded because, hello? Girls at every stop? Who wouldn't like that? But I guess this last year has been weird. The guys have been finding girlfriends, and I didn't really notice it happening at all. One minute we were all playing World of

Warcraft every night, and next time I looked up, they were coupled off."

Yeah. Weird. In truth, he'd been so stressed about protecting Will, he wouldn't have noticed if the freaking country had been taken over by aliens.

"So everyone has a girlfriend now?" she said.

"Except Nathan and me, I think. I don't know really." He started to backtrack. "Remember we don't want to talk about it, though, so it's off the record." Last thing he needed was being quoted as saying none of the guys were available. Be a fucking nightmare if he kept his brother from being fired all these months, only to get canned because of some young reporter. At least, she *looked* young. "How old are you anyway?"

She looked away. Huh. Was she really super-old? Super-young?

"What's the matter? Cat got your...age? Wait. Are you, like, fifty?"

Her head spun around, and her mouth gaped open. *Score*.

"What? Fifty? I look fifty?" And then she clocked his grin and punched his arm again. He let her this time.

"No. How old are you, really?"

"I don't know what to say. When I turned up, Natasha told me that LJ insisted on everyone being over twenty-five...I don't know...because he didn't want anyone to be tempted to do anything bad with you guys, I think."

First he'd heard of an age restriction for the workers. But for once, LJ had maybe had the right idea. Because Matt was finding it very, very hard not to fantasize about just what sort of bad things he could do with Anya.

"So we'll do a whole 'don't ask don't tell' thing about

your age then," he said.

"Deal." She looked so relieved that a small concern about her age lodged itself in his head. Hmmm.

"So maybe you don't say anything about us having to stay single, and I won't mention your age to anyone. But you should feel free to say that Miles is gay."

She grinned at him. "I'm not going to say that."

"Oh, go on. I'll let you off one of your dares." he said.

"What dares?" She frowned. "I don't remember any dares."

"This evening you're watching the show from the podium at the side of the stage. If I look at you and don't see you dancing, you owe me a dare. I know I'm going to get at least three or four per show, so I'll let you off one. That's all."

Her mouth twisted and her eyes narrowed into an "I'm going to get you" expression.

"Here we are." The car passed the screaming girls and security waved them through. They pulled up outside The One and got out. "I've got to spend the rest of the day getting ready and psyching up for the show. Meet me afterward?"

"Okay. Are you looking forward to it?"

Meeting her? He furrowed his brow. "Forward to…?"

"The show," she said, heaving her bag onto her shoulder.

"Oh right. Yeah. That too." He watched her blush and winked at her as he slammed the door.

She spun on her feet like a dancer, paused, and then walked off to Hanging On. Truth be told, he'd rather like to hang on to her. She was a puzzle. The more she said, the less he understood about her. But every time they were together, he felt like they were on a date. And when they'd been so close… *So* close in that dark changing room—he swallowed, watching her disappear into her bus—there'd definitely been trouser tenting.

God only knew how he'd have been able to control himself if he'd actually kissed her. He'd been so ready to seal the deal, but it'd been so dark, he hadn't wanted to risk passionately kissing her chin or nose. There really wasn't any walking it back from French kissing a nose. He was proud of his restraint.

He rolled his eyes at himself and stepped up into the bus. Opposite the door was a makeup and costuming schedule. He was up first. Joy. That meant he was the one who'd have to sit around in full stage makeup and their itchy first costume for three hours.

The guys were fighting. Again. As much as everyone had mellowed and become better humored the last month or so, on show day, tensions and emotions always ran high. In his cheat book, Will had warned him not to mess with Ryder on show day. He was the antsiest of all of them. And even when he wasn't, he was the one most likely to tour-rage someone.

"I swear to God, if you don't take that tweet down, *right now*, tweeting is the only sound you'll be able to make tonight. Understand?" Ryder had Miles by his collar, his fist drawn back as if he was ready to explode.

"Relax," Trevin said from the sofa. "He didn't really tweet it. It's his private account. We're the only ones who can see that one. Look, it's the account with the padlock."

"You better be fucking right." Ryder dropped Miles and looked at his own phone. "Okay. Don't fuck with me again, dickhead. Otherwise I'm just going to punch first and ask questions later."

"Take a pill…it was just a joke." Miles grinned.

Matt had no idea how they all managed to stay sane

in one bus together. Sometimes it was good bonding time, sometimes they were ticking time bombs. And it wasn't so easy to get off when you're going seventy down a highway. In a bus with your half-naked body plastered down the side. He flipped open a galley cupboard and grabbed a file with Miles's headshots. He took one off the top.

"Here. Sign this to"—he pulled the card from his pocket—"to Chris." Perfect. He'd totally think it was a girl. "You owe me for dumping me at the shelter."

Miles smiled mildly. "You know that wasn't my idea. But it's nice to know someone wants *my* signed photo. I'm the heartthrob, you know."

Matt grinned. Miles sometimes liked to try to rile the others with his heartthrob status. He was only playing with them, though. He was definitely not the type to think he was really irresistible.

The guys all threw whatever they had in their hands. In two seconds, Miles had half a sub sandwich, a book, and a remote control in his lap after they'd all bounced off his head. "Suck it, losers," he said, grabbing the photo and uncapping a pen with his teeth.

Matt watched as he wrote "I love you, Chris" before signing his name. He wanted to laugh so badly, but no sense in rocking the boat, especially when it wasn't his boat.

"Cheers, mate," Matt said in an imitation of Miles's English accent. "Maybe we should all go onstage and speak to the audience in Miles's accent tonight, since everyone loves him."

"Great idea, sport," Nathan said in his well-practiced takeoff of Miles.

"For fuck's sake, guys," Miles protested, but barely. He

was smiling at something on his phone. A little while ago he would have had his face in Matt's face demanding an apology, but since he hooked up with one of the roadies' sisters he'd been a pussy.

For a minute, Matt wondered what it would be like to be so into someone else that pathetic jibes and sneers became mere smears on the windshield of life. Must be nice. Couldn't imagine it himself, though.

. . .

Anya sat alone in the Hanging On bus trying to figure out how to charge the tablet WowSounds had sent. She'd never actually used a tablet before the previous day, so she was still a little shaky on how it all worked.

Eventually she got it booted up and hooked up to an outlet by the TV. She logged on to the site and opened the previous night's blog. Holy crap. That couldn't be right, could it? There were over a thousand comments. She paged down. Wow. There were a lot of questions. And double-wow: some people were so rude. And frightening.

You're a bitch, and if you lay one hand on Will Fray, I will kill you. I know where you live.

Hah! Doubtful.

They all have STDs. Better not touch any of them, they're losers.

Well, not total losers if they all got laid, she supposed.

I've got a question. Ask Miles why he doesn't reply to my letters and presents.

Anya shuddered. She hated to think what kind of presents they got in the mail. Maybe she could ask someone and get into that for a blog post.

Some people asked legit questions that she could pose to Will. She jotted them down in her notebook so she could ask him tomorrow. He'd probably be too tired after the show.

An icon on the bottom toolbar was flashing. An envelope. She clicked on it and a whole email account popped up. Anya.Anderson@wowsounds.com. Cool. She had a "work" email account. She sat up straighter, suddenly feeling as if she had a real job like a real, proper adult.

She had five emails. Four were about office stuff: keeping the photocopy room clean, a potluck lunch, a missing stapler, and the last informing everyone that the missing stapler had in fact been found "shaken, but okay." She grinned. She didn't know any of them, but they sounded so friendly to one another, suddenly she wanted to be part of their office family...

Then she clicked on the one from her editor, Cynthia Wilcox.

Dear Mrs. Anderson,

I hope you received your tablet—I'm guessing you did or you wouldn't be reading this email. Your first blog post was great and garnered more page hits than we'd seen since the spate of tornados we had a couple of years ago. So as of last night, you're my top reporter in the field! If you fill in the attached document with your bank account details, SSN etc., I can have a one hundred dollar per diem wired to your account. I will also try to come and meet you in person, either here or in New Orleans, depending on my schedule.

Best wishes,

Cyn.

Bank account? *Yeah right.* She'd have to hope she could

talk them into a check again. It had never even crossed her mind that people got paid directly into bank accounts. Mr. Patel, who owned the tiny grocery store on 15th Street, had allowed her to have her mail sent to him and had cashed the check for the homeless article. Maybe he'd let her open an account using his address.

And then there was the whole meeting up thing. Hopefully that wouldn't happen. She was sure Cynthia would see immediately that she was young. Like too young to be a writer or a legal employee or something. And once that happened, there would be no money. Not a *per diem*, whatever that was, and not a biggest-scoop-of-the-decade fee.

She quickly Googled it. What? *Per diem* was an amount paid daily for expenses? Daily? One hundred dollars a day? Blood rushed away from her head and she lay back on the booth. One hundred dollars a day? If she could string out this job she might be able to save enough for a couple of months at a motel. Maybe things were looking up.

Grabbing her notebook, she flipped to the page of Will facts. She added:

Needle phobia—passes out!
Alice Singleton first girlfriend
Will and Nathan the only singles left on the tour.

After doodling a little on the page, she shut the book and drafted her post for the evening and scheduled it to post at ten p.m. That would allow her time to change it after the show if she wanted. The show. Her mind flittered to Will, nuzzling her neck in the changing room. Holding her hand. Heat spread through her in an uncomfortable way.

She dragged her mind back to the show. She'd have to dance. Urgh. She had no idea if she could dance, or even if she danced right. She hadn't seen anyone dance since she was at home. And that had only been watching movies about prom. She probably still danced like a thirteen-year-old. And then she wondered what the dares were going to be. Anxiety pushed up through the layer of ease she hadn't even noticed until now. Until it was being pushed aside.

Well, he didn't say she had to dance well. She closed her eyes and took a deep breath, then another, and another…

"Are you all right?" a voice shouted.

Anya started and sat up, whacking her knee against the table where she'd fallen asleep. "Ow. What?"

Natasha was swinging in the doorway, half in and half out. "Are you coming for the concert? It's starting in a sec."

Anya looked out of the window. Dusk had fallen. Jeez, how long had she been asleep? "I'm up. I'm coming."

"I swear to God, you must be the only person here so bored that you fall asleep on a rock tour!" she said, giggling. "Come on. We won't get pole position on the podium unless we go now."

"Pole what?" Anya said, half standing and then banging her head on the cabinet above the booth. "Ow."

"Seriously? Come on. Get it together. You weren't in a coma."

She was right. She was used to going from sleep to running in a split second. She was losing her edge. Two days off the street and she was losing her ability to stay safe. "I'm coming." She shoved the tablet into her bunk and ran down the length of the bus to Natasha. "Okay. I'm ready."

Natasha rolled her eyes and slammed the door shut behind them. "Were you at least having a nice dream?"

"I don't remember. I don't even remember falling asleep." She was so freaking busted. Never, ever would she have fallen asleep in the past without fixing her surroundings. But it did fit with her sleep schedule. On the streets, she tried to stay awake at night and sleep during the day. It was less dangerous.

Music came from the stadium. "Did they start already?" Anya asked, picking up speed.

"Oh no. that's just the opening band. Sister Act. I mean, that's not their name. They're the ones who we avoided in the makeup trailer yesterday. Their band name is Cherry. We call them Sister Act just to piss them off. Well, to piss off the older sister, anyway. Paige. She's a total bitch. Do not get in between her and a mirror."

"Huh?"

She whispered, "We think the mirror talks to her. In a 'find Snow White and kill her' way."

They both giggled.

"The band has several opening acts, but they're already the most famous, so they go on just before S2J," she explained. Natasha smoothed down her skirt as she walked. She was wearing a sparkly mini skirt and an off-the-shoulder baggy T-shirt that showed a racer-back tank underneath.

Anya wished she'd had time to change into something more concerty. Except she didn't really have anything more concerty. She'd amassed six outfits from stuff she'd grabbed before the bailiffs had taken everything, from homeless shelter donations, and last week she'd bought her denim skirt from a thrift store for $7.50 out of her pay for the article she wrote. It had felt impossibly extravagant at the time. Now? Maybe not.

Well, with twenty thousand screaming fans in one arena, she was sure no one, least of all Will, would be looking at what she was wearing.

Natasha led her through the same maze of backstage corridors Will had taken her through, and like him, she busted through the door of the catering room. She also called it the greenroom, although there was nothing green about it. Especially food-wise. It was all fried or sugary, or both. "You want something before we go up?" Natasha asked, her head already down over the buffet, filling up a shiny white plate.

Of course she did. Crap. Again she hadn't brought her bag to stash food. But it felt like this spread was always here. Anya took hunks of freshly baked seeded bread, knowing it would fill her up more than the chips and dip. She added slices of cheese and ham to her plate, sat on the same sofa she and Will had collapsed on, and chowed down on the huge sandwich.

Cheering and whistles threaded their way through the stadium corridors to the greenroom. Anya looked at Natasha, wondering if they'd have time to finish their food.

"Don't worry. It's Jim, one of the sound guys. They always send him onstage about twenty minutes before the guys to gauge the crowd, get them excited. All he does is check that the instruments are plugged firmly into the amplifiers. It's the high point of his day…until this happens. Wait for it…"

A second later, boos throbbed through the walls. Anya grinned.

"Yup, they just realized he wasn't one of the guys and is in fact a middle-aged man," Natasha said with a mouth full of something.

They fell silent as they finished eating. Natasha took her plate and chucked her a really big bottle of water. "Take it with you. It'll be hot and sweaty out there, and you better stay hydrated or you'll regret it."

"Yes, mom," Anya said without thinking. *Oh shit. What the what?*

"The nerve of you!" Natasha replied shoving her nose in the air a bit. And then she grinned. "Well someone's got to look after the newb." Holding the door open for Anya, she continued, "Of course, some newbs are more brattish than others." She elbowed Anya as she passed, and Anya elbowed her back until they were both squished in the door-frame together, trying to get out.

They giggled and pushed into the corridor.

As the door swung behind them, a raucous thumping shook the floor and the walls around them. The audience were stomping their feet.

"Oh hurry," Natasha said. "They do that in time to the light display. It counts down to the band's arrival onstage." She grabbed Anya's hand and hurried through a door and past several blackout curtains and up some metal stairs. The podium. Four people were already on it, but two of them had headphone/mikes on, so they probably weren't there for the view. Natasha dragged her to the front of the elevated section overlooking the stage.

Anya held on to the metal bar in front of her as the stomping feet of the crowd made the platform shake. With each stomp came a lightning flash on the stage. The lights got faster and faster until there was a loud explosion and they stayed on, sweeping the stage with bright light.

A second later, the five guys sprung out from under the stage, literally being flung upward by some kind of mechanism. The crowd went absolutely nuts. Screaming and shouting and cheering and clapping and stomping.

Anya couldn't even hear the music, but as her heart thumped with every beat of the crowd, she started smiling. Then grinning, and then as the music finally made itself heard, bobbing up and down. It was like she had no control of her body. The music was louder than anything she'd heard before. The darkness of the backstage area, the heat of the lights from the stage, and the contagious emotion of the crowd… It filled her with such strange impulses.

She wanted to cry, to dance, to jump up and down. She looked for Natasha. Her eyes were shining and she seemed about to explode just like Anya. They caught each other's eyes and impulsively hugged, virtually levitating with happiness. It was euphoric.

When she got a little more used to the feelings flooding through her, she searched the stage for Will. He was on the opposite side of the stage to her, in front of a static mike attached to a pole. All the guys had their left hands on their own stands and were pushing them away, toward the audience as if to get them to sing into them. They complied. Anya wished she knew the words to the songs, too. Then they stepped on the base of the mike stands to flip them back in one choreographed move that made everyone scream again.

They were incredible. She'd literally never seen anything like it before. Not ever. She could just as well have been looking at an alien invasion, it was so new to her. As the band stomped their way across the stage in time to the music, her heart felt as if it was beating out of her chest.

Twice Will came to the side of the stage and met her eyes, and each time a rush of exhilaration flooded through her. The grin he gave her was enough to make her want to jump off the podium and stake her claim right then and there.

She had no words for what was happening to her, except it felt like Jude's description of being high.

A slow song began and the audience held their phones up and swayed them in time to the music. It was a beautiful sight, like fireflies dancing in the dark.

Then Ryder, the one covered in tattoos, took the mike and said in a terrible British accent, "Who here wants to get wet?" Suddenly, she knew it must be the end of the show. The crowd shrieked and Anya wondered if they knew exactly what he was asking of them.

"I can't believe you're not taking photos!" Natasha yelled.

"I didn't bring my camera," she shouted back. Natasha was right, it was a shame.

"Next time. Or just bring your tablet." She made a square outline with her fingers.

Oh. Right. It probably had a camera attached. She nodded. "Next time," she said, turning back to the stage.

As the opening bars to "WET" came on, a huge archway untethered from the back of the stage and slowly cruised forward, until it almost blocked her sight. She shuffled to her left so she could see better, making Natasha laugh. "So you've heard this is the hottest number of the show!"

Transfixed, Anya stared at the full theatrical number she'd seen only in rehearsal. Thunder and crackling lightning came over the loudspeakers. Then lights flashed and the rain poured down on the band, soaking them instantly. Will was now second-closest to her, and she watched as he grinned with unbelievable confidence for a shy guy. Except she didn't buy his shyness one iota. Not with the way he moved. It was like his true self was waiting inside, hidden, and he could only let it out onstage. His blue shirt was plastered to his chest as he spun, and water flew out in a circle from his hair. She gasped, and her hand flew to her chest. He looked… *awesome? Sexy? Totally hot*? Ahem. He looked all right.

He caught her eye again, and she could have sworn he'd winked at her. She was light-headed with feelings she couldn't fully find the words to explain.

The music pulsed as they sang, kicking water into the crowd, and at one another, looking as if they were having a ball. Suddenly she wanted to be there, kicking water at them, having fun. It was hypnotic. The whole concert was hypnotic.

The music died, and the boys left the stage, blowing kisses and bowing. She knew she had to go rewrite her post for the night. Nothing in her seventeen years had prepared her for the way she'd responded to the music, the crowd, the energy.

"I've got to go back and write my blog post!" Anya shouted to Natasha.

She shook her head. "No! You'll miss the best bit!"

"What best bit? It's over," she yelled.

"You're going to want to see Will now!"

"Why? Won't he be tired?" She frowned. She really did need to go intercept that bland post. She wondered if she'd find the words to explain how awesome the evening had been.

"Are you kidding? He'll be so hyped-up, you'll probably need to keep a leash on him. They all will be. It's fun!"

A shot of reality oozed through her veins. Hyped-up was uncontrollable. Hyped-up was dangerous. But she wasn't on the streets. She was safe here, surely.

She figured she would spend maybe half an hour with him, and then she'd still have time to rewrite her post.

• • •

Post from the tour.

I saw my first proper Seconds to Juliet show tonight. Yes, I'd seen a short rehearsal of the famous finale. Yes, I knew that the show would be sexy—it'd have to be, right? With all you ladies (and gentlemen—admit it, I saw you screaming, too) seemingly obsessed with the boys in the band. And I have to say… It was pretty good. I may have even stopped dancing for a moment just to appreciate the vision onstage. I hear they don't do this finale, this special finale that I am duty bound not to divulge (yes, you'll have to see it yourself if you want to be showered in the glory of S2J) in every show. So if you get to experience it, you are truly special, too.

Meanwhile, if your name is Alice Singleton and you dated a football player in high school…I bet you're kicking yourself right now. AmIrite?

Chapter Nine

Matt bounced off the stage, barely managing to stay on his feet. The buzz of adulation zinged through him like lightning through a power line.

"Yeah!" he shouted to no one.

"Fucking A, dude." Miles high-fived him and totally missed, nearly smacking him in the head. They laughed like they'd just seen the funniest thing in Funnyville on national funny day.

He'd never get tired of this feeling. The pure adrenaline rush when they came offstage.

Ryder was punching the air, dancing like he was a prize-fighter.

"What are we going to do tonight, guys?" Nathan asked, flushed and bouncing off the walls.

"You were so fucking good, Nath." Matt rubbed the poor guy's cheeks with the palms of his hands. "Hell, we were all on fire."

"We killed, man. It was sick!" Ryder shouted. "You even remembered the fucking words, shy guy."

The swearing didn't stop until LJ came in and nodded approvingly. "Good show, boys. Good show. Now go get dry and get some sleep. I'm leaving tonight for New Orleans. I'll see you there tomorrow evening."

"Night, LJ," the guys' voices rumbled round the room, but Matt couldn't bring himself to be polite to him when he didn't absolutely have to.

They had a free night. A totally free night. Most often when they changed venues, they got on the bus immediately after the last curtain call and headed off. The Tulsa police had asked if they could leave in the morning so they didn't have to assign the whole night shift to making sure they got safely away. Which meant they had the whole night to make mischief, because they could sleep on the road.

Except mischief had been pretty hard to come by since it seemed that three of the five guys only wanted to get on the phones with their significant others in the evening.

When the phones came out, he decided to bail and look for Anya. He counted like five times she hadn't been dancing. Maybe she hated the music, but he intended to tally those dares and use them to his advantage. Maybe to avoid questions that may out him. But hell, right now he felt like he totally had his shit together. He was one of the band. Even the other three had no idea he wasn't Will.

Natasha was in the corridor talking to Nick, one of the tech guys. She caught his eye and stuck out a fist. "Great show."

"Thanks," he said, bumping her fist.

"Killed," Nick nodded.

"Thanks, man. Hey, have either of you seen Anya?"

"She went back to Hanging On to do something with a blog post. Save it? Stop it? Something." She slurped on the straw in her cocktail.

"Thanks."

He ran out of the arena building and back to the buses. Suddenly, he just wanted to see her, to make sure she liked the show. To see what she was writing.

Should he be concerned about why she wanted to change a blog post? Should he take her a drink? Maybe she didn't drink. None of them should probably drink. Maybe he should take her something else? Food? Flowers?

Wait…what?

Jesus—his brain was fritzing as fast as his heart was. It was the high. Will had warned him not to do anything impulsive after a show. But obviously Will didn't understand. Matt could handle it.

He ran into Hanging On, taking the steps in one bound, slamming the door open with such force the whole bus rocked.

Anya was there, virtually clinging to the ceiling. As soon as the door banged, he saw that he had totally spooked her. She'd jumped up and both hands had gone around her head. She was seriously jumpy.

"Sorry, it's just me. I couldn't find you. Do you want a drink? Did you like the show?" *Shit, slow down, buddy.*

She sank back into the booth that she'd been sitting at. He slid in opposite her. "What are you doing?"

"The blog already posted to the site. It's kinda pathetic really. I'm going to have to write a whole other piece to make up for how…bland this one is. I wrote it before I saw the show."

"You what? Seriously? You just posted about something before it happened?" He frowned at her. Journalism didn't work that way, right?

Anya dropped her head to the table and banged it gently. Once, twice, and she was obviously going for a third time, so he slipped his hand between her forehead and the tabletop, cushioning her despair.

She let her head rest on his hand, and something in him slid. Something changed.

He lifted her head and scrambled out of the booth, his hand still on her face. He crouched beside her, lowered his mouth to her cherry-red lips, and kissed her. He teased her lips open under his. She moaned into his mouth as his tongue touched hers. Heat flickered through his body, igniting a fuse in him that he couldn't tamp down.

Except she shoved him away. Like, hard. He toppled over onto his ass, and she jumped up, pacing the short carpet between the galley kitchen and the booths.

"What was that? What the hell was that? You can't just go around kissing random people without notice. It's rude. You're rude." She paced more, and he smiled. She was as jacked as he was.

He sprung up. "Sorry. I'm flying on adrenaline. I...don't know what came over me. But whatever it was, it's catching." He paused as she stalked up and down the bus. "Are you fixing to wear a hole in the rug?"

She stopped in front of him, a look of utter bewilderment in her eyes. Hell, he wanted to kiss her again. Instead he held out his hand. "Let's get out of here. We need some air."

Without speaking, she swiped some strands of hair off

her face and nodded. She looked at his hand for a good three seconds, and he was about to drop it when she took it. When she gazed into his eyes for an instant, he slipped further into…what? He'd been around the block with his share of girls, but he'd never felt something like this.

He lowered his eyes, scared that she would see something in them that he didn't have a name for, and swallowed. Then he raised his head, forced a grin, and ran out of the bus, dragging her behind him.

They rushed back into the building, but as soon as they got through the door, he took a sharp right, up the backstage emergency exit stairs. He ran with her until they reached the very top and he pushed through the door.

"Wow," Anya breathed, still panting from the exertion.

"I love roofs. So close to the stars. So far above everyone else." He laughed as he sat, shimmying forward until his legs dangled off the roof, and his arms hung over the metal guardrail. She sat next to him, threading her arms around the rail, too. "Don't fall, I'm not sure our insurance will cover it."

"I'll try not to," she said in a dry tone.

He caught her eye, relieved to see she was smiling.

He lay back so he was looking up at the stars. Will was lucky to have this. It had been an amazing experience for Matt, and if Will came back and looked after his career properly, he would always have this. And that made Matt happy he'd agreed to cover for him. Not that he had much choice. But still. It had been so cool so far to live the life a little, along with the option to fade away, back to being "brother of the star."

"Penny for your thoughts?" Anya said, lying back next

to him.

"I wish I knew what all the stars were. I feel like it would be a good pickup line right now if I could name them all."

She raised her arm and pointed to a cluster of stars. "See that one? That's Orion. He's a warrior. You can see his armor, and his belt, and if you look at his shoulder, in your peripheral vision you can see the dagger hanging from his belt."

Was she serious? "That's awesome. Show me another." How cool was she anyway?

"That one, shaped like a cooking pan is called the Great Bear, or the Big Dipper. The sides of the pan…there"—she pointed straight up—they point directly to the North Star, the star by which all the ancient sailors navigated."

Huh. He rolled onto one elbow. "I was right."

"What do you mean? Right about what?"

"It's an awesome pickup line."

• • •

Anya's heart hadn't stopped thumping through her chest since he'd kissed her. She didn't know what had made him do that. But she wanted to make him do it again. Her first kiss. That is if you didn't count Jimmy Madden in fifth grade, and she didn't. She used to, but not now. Not as of ten minutes ago. Now she knew what a real kiss was like.

She rolled up onto her side, too, and searched his eyes for something, she didn't know what. But it was so dark up there, she couldn't really see anything other than the outline of him.

He spoke first. "Sorry about kissing you before. It was the

adrenaline after the show. It's still in me. But when I get off the stage, I feel like I can fly. Like my body isn't big enough to hold everything inside me. Like I'm going to explode." He paused and flung himself on his back again and reached his arms up toward the sky and stretched. "Hey, we can just be thankful that it was you there, and not LJ, right?"

Her heart rolled over and curled into a dry ball of what-the-hell. So he would have kissed an old man if she hadn't been there? What a jerk! There she had been, basking in her first kiss, and she could have been anyone at all. Anyone that just happened to be in reach. What a —

"That is, if you hated it and never want me to kiss you again. If, by a complete shot in the dark, you actually liked it, then I have to say…" He rolled over again and poked her kind of hard in the ribs. "I'd certainly prefer to kiss you than LJ. Well, almost certainly."

Jerk!

"Whaaat?" Relief and outrage spiked together and she jumped on top of him, making him "Ooof." She jabbed her fingers into his ribs as he tried in vain to catch her hands. "I'm interchangeable with LJ, am I? Maybe I should kiss him and let you know what it's like, huh?"

He grabbed her wrists and levered himself so he was sitting again, leaving her astride his lap. "Stop. Come here," he whispered, leaning in to her.

She met him halfway, her eyes fluttering shut as his mouth caressed her jaw. She stretched her neck to allow him better access. The breeze fluttering across the roof mimicked his lips grazing over her face. He pulled away slightly and, after a second, she opened her eyes to see him staring at her. He slowly tucked a piece of hair behind her ear. "You're beautiful," he said simply.

She looked away from him, unwilling to accept that he was being truthful. Fingers tipped her chin back up, and his lips slowly sunk to hers. She felt as if she were melting, from her legs, to her stomach, to her brain that no longer held a thought. For a few minutes, her whole world became Will, and his kiss.

He pulled away and moaned, "LJ," against her cheek. He ducked away, laughing before she could reach him with her poking fingers again.

She giggled, rolling off his lap and jumping to her feet. They were so alone up here, it was as if they were in their own world. She leaned over the railing. "Look. People are still down there." They seemed as much like specks as the stars above them.

He joined her and looked down. "There are always some stragglers." He pointed at some men on the stage. "They'll be breaking down the set for about five hours, and then they'll transport it to our next stop. Come seven a.m., it'll be like we were never here. Sometimes it feels as if we're a mirage. Not really anywhere."

There was silence for a moment as they watched the people below them, while she was blissfully aware that one of the most famous boys in the world was watching them. With her. A homeless girl with nothing. She waited for the familiar anxiety to prod its way back inside her, but she felt nothing except the excitement of being with Will, and having him kiss her like that.

"So. I have something important to tell you." He turned so his back was leaning against the metal barrier, his face solemn. "I watched you during the show, and I counted five times that you weren't dancing. Which means you owe me five dares."

Something twisted in her stomach as she wondered what he might ask her to do. Still no anxiety. "Well maybe I'll just ask for my money back, because obviously if there were a whole five times that I wasn't dancing, you can't have been that good."

"That argument would hold a lot more water if you'd, you know, actually *paid for your ticket*." He crossed his arms and nudged her.

"True," she allowed.

"You did like it though, right?" He sounded a tiny bit unsure.

Something loud clanged from the stage, echoing around the stadium and up toward them. They both turned toward the sound, and Anya jumped as he slipped his arm around her.

"How did you ever get the reputation of being the shy one of the band? You could be the least shy person I've ever met," she said, smiling to herself. Maybe she had found out something about him. Not really a scoop, though.

His arm fell away and he took a step back. He didn't say anything for a moment and she looked at him kicking the dirt and hanging his head. "Okay, so you're painfully shy." She laughed at his pathetic playacting. "So what's my first dare?"

"I haven't decided yet, but the night is still young, isn't it?"

"I don't know, I don't have a watch," she replied, wondering what the time was.

"Well I'm going to keep you up until the sun rises. We'll

sleep when we're dead." He threw his arms up like he'd just scored a goal and spun around looking up at the sky.

She shook her head. "What are we going to do?" She wondered what exactly he had in mind. Drinking? More kissing? More than that? What if he used his dares to get her to do something…sexy?

"First of all, we're going to play Uno. Do you know how to play?"

What? "Um, maybe? I think I last played when I was maybe seven?"

"That's awesome. You'll be easy to beat. Stay here. I'll be back in ten minutes. Don't go anywhere." He ran for the exit door, hesitated with his hand on the handle, turned around, and ran back to her. He grabbed her around the waist and planted a kiss on her lips. "Ten minutes, okay? Don't forget me." He ran off again.

"Don't forget *me*," she said to the swinging door.

Chapter Ten

Twenty minutes later, Matt was already bored with playing Uno. He was pacing the roof. "You want to go back to my bus?" he asked. *Did that sound bad? That sounded bad.*

"No. You told me that wasn't allowed."

"That's true." He continued to pace.

"Can I ask you some stuff? For my posts?" She stood up and tried to keep in step with him. "Why don't we go down and walk around the arena? Do you think that might help?"

Eh. Couldn't hurt. "Sure. I guess. Everyone's probably gone by now anyway."

They went back down the stairs and hit the parking lot that surrounded the venue. They slipped into a pace halfway between stopped dead and an amble.

Anya broke the silence. "So what kind of gifts do girls send you? I got a comment on the post saying that you never replied to this girl who sent you presents and letters."

"Oh my God. *Anya.* You should know better than to

read the comments. For the same reason that we don't get shown the letters and gifts unless they're from people we know. No good comes of it." He slowed down a bit, suddenly worried. "What else did they say?"

"Someone threatened to kill me if I laid a hand on Will Fray."

That brought him to a stop. "What?"

"They said that they know where I live." She smiled as if she didn't care.

"Is there a chance they do know where you live?" he asked. "Should I get Beau on this?"

"Who's Beau?" she asked, continuing to walk. He stayed still.

"He leads our security detail. Hey. Come back."

She stopped then and realized how far behind her he was. She returned and stood so close to him that the tips of her toes were touching his. In the light of the parking lot's floodlights, her hair looked navy blue, it was so black. And her eyes sparkled with a lighter blue. She took his breath away. Literally. She tipped her head to one side.

"What's the matter? Don't you get death threats from crazy girls all the time? I'm not scared of a girl on a computer. I'd be scared of a girl without a computer, someone with nothing to lose."

Suddenly he realized he didn't know her at all. Like, *at all*. "Who are you, Anya?" he asked as he tucked her floating hair behind her ear. Every time she was within reach, he wanted to touch her hair. Her eyes widened very slightly.

"I'm just me." Her tongue darted out and licked a tiny place on her bottom lip. Jesus, she was sexy. He'd literally never met anyone so…interesting. Except he had no idea if she was interesting. Maybe she was completely boring.

"Tell me something about you. Why do you always wear your hair up? Why haven't I ever seen you with a cell phone? Where do you live? Where are you from originally? Cats or dogs? Homebody or wanderluster?" He was kind of aware that he sounded desperate, and he wasn't sure why.

"Wow." She took a step away. "Where would you like me to start?"

He swallowed and tried to cover it with a laugh. "Your first dare. Take your hair out of its…whatever keeps it up there."

A frown briefly touched her beautiful face. Then she shrugged and smiled. "Good thing I washed it this morning." She drew some long pins from her hair and stuffed them in her pocket. Her hair was shoulder length, choppy. Probably an expensive hairdresser made it look as if it had been hacked off on a desert island.

He reclaimed the step she had taken backward and touched her hair with his finger first. Just one finger on one shiny lock. Her eyes closed and he realized that he'd shoved his whole hand into her hair and was smoothing it from her head to the ends. It felt like silk. Heavy cool silk. "It feels incredible."

He tightened his grasp on it, tugging her hair ever so lightly, pulling her head to one side. Her eyes fluttered closed, and he kissed her. Because he could. Because there was no way he couldn't. And then his other hand was on her head, bringing her closer. He needed her closer. Every kiss they had made him want her more. Need her presence. Her stillness.

"Will? Is that you, Will?" He heard the words, but they

just didn't register. Anya pulled away, ducking her head as if embarrassed to be caught kissing him.

"Will?" Yeah. He was Will.

"Mrs. Carlisle?"

"I think it's time for this young lady to say good night, don't you? The buses will be leaving in about an hour."

Shoot me now. "Yes ma'am. Just taking her back."

"Okay then. Have a good night." She went off toward the buses.

"Who was that?" Anya asked as he slipped his hand in hers and followed Miles's mom.

"She's one of the parents. She acts as a chaperone. Everyone under the age of eighteen has to have a raft of them on tour to keep us on the straight and narrow."

"That makes sense, I guess," she replied.

"It's a pain in the ass," he mumbled.

She didn't reply. He walked her to the Hanging On bus and kissed her hand like some idiot knight of the roundtable. What was the matter with him? But the smile that spread across her face as she turned to go…maybe he should try to be more knightly? She disappeared into the bus, and he kicked himself. This wasn't a relationship. This was…a means to an end or something. He was distracting her from her interviews. That was all.

That was all.

• • •

Natasha was still out, so Anya had the bus to herself. Maybe she was with her relatives in that swanky hotel she'd mentioned. So it would be just her and the driver going to New

Orleans? That felt weird to be alone with a man at night. Maybe she should try to stay awake. She should be used to staying awake in the night, but this schedule was messing up her usual routine.

She extracted her notebook from under her pillow and went to the section on Will, finding it quickly as it was the most worn page.

Likes high places. Likes roofs.

Not really shy, but doesn't like it being pointed out.

Instead of getting in her bunk, she booted up the tablet. It did indeed have a camera. She experimented with taking photos and took one of the driver getting on the bus. He acted like a pilot. He attached a see-through map to his visor and called in over a radio to all the other buses doing a radio check.

"The One. Loud and clear."

"Not Tonight. Loud and clear."

And so it went on down to the ones that didn't have song names, just numbers. She counted fifteen. Suddenly she didn't feel so alone.

Her last, slightly premature, blog post had over three hundred comments already. As she read one, she realized she was going to have to put out another post right now.

Really? The concert was "pretty good"? What are you even doing there if you're not a fan?

Whoever *Anon98* was, they were right. She had to be a fan here. She had to let the commenters feel as if they were experiencing what she was experiencing. And she had experienced a lot over the past day. He mind wandered to the first time Will kissed her, the first time she'd been kissed. The first time she'd felt anything other than fear and anxiety in years. And it was knee-wobblingly good. Her heart pumped faster even just thinking about it.

The blog post came flying out of her fingers. Everything she'd felt during the concert, everything she wanted to know about them, and everything she vowed to find out for the fans who read WowSounds.

Once it had been posted, she sat back and allowed herself to think about Will again. She promised herself she would try to find out more about him. He seemed very good at evading questions and not talking about himself. Clearly that wasn't going to cut it if she was going to get some kind of scoop. Mind you, even the money she was getting as her per diem would help. But not if she wanted to get Jude off the streets, too. And she really did. She'd only really realized how much she needed to help him when she'd lost him.

He'd literally saved her life the first week she'd ditched her first and last foster home. She'd kept her head down as she passed him like she did with everyone, but something made her turn back. He'd stopped and was watching her with a totally blank face. It had scared her, so she'd sped up and dipped into an alley. Worst mistake of her short life.

Three men had been in the alleyway, exchanging something between them, and when they'd seen her, they'd come alive. Without hesitating, they crowded around her, asking her name, touching her hair. She'd closed her eyes, not knowing how she could get away and hoping she would die right then so that she'd never know what those men might do to her. Almost immediately, she heard a grunting sound. Jude was hitting the men. Kicking them and hitting them in moves she'd only ever seen on TV.

"Run," he'd said as one of the three men made to get up

again.

She'd ran but waited at the next corner for him. When he emerged, he'd walked straight past her as if she hadn't existed. Running to keep up with his long strides, she tried to thank him, but he wouldn't talk to her. Didn't even seem to know she was there. Eventually he slowed down and started shaking. Like a fever of 103 shaking.

He'd started rambling and muttering about things she didn't understand. Feeling responsible for whatever was happening to him, she ushered him into an underground parking lot, where he curled up in a concrete corner. She'd just sat herself down next to him and slept for the first time in two days.

Anya shook herself out of the trip down memory lane. That had been nearly two years ago. He'd shown her how to exist on the streets and never asked her anything about why she was there. She, in turn, didn't ask anything about him, either, but had found out later from the shelter that he was a veteran. She owed him. Now more than ever. Now she was safe and warm in a bus with endless food and drink. She clenched her fists. She would make this work so she could get both of them off the streets.

The bus doors swooshed and Natasha jumped on. "Made it!" she said, breathing hard.

"Only just," Anya said in a way that made it sound like Natasha was always there at the last minute. For a second, she worried Natasha would take it the wrong way, but the girl smiled. Maybe Natasha really had meant it when she declared them instant friends.

Natasha threw herself on the seat opposite Anya. "So how goes it?"

"Fine, thank you. Where have you been?"

"My family blew me off, claiming jet lag, so I hung out with Nick. He's a college boy. And oh man, I love how college boys kiss." She smiled dreamily.

Anya laughed. "Wow. Do you like him?"

"Sure, today I do. We have tour rules here. What happens on tour, stays on tour. So no forever relationships. Hah! More like relation-ships that pass in the night."

"How many people have you kissed since the tour started?" Anya asked, genuinely interested in the shenanigans. Maybe she could write about the behind-the-scenes people, too.

"Lost count, sweetie. Let's see. There was Danny in publicity, I guess"—she counted on her fingers—"three roadies: Steve, Matt, and Ryan, and of course, my first was Will."

Anya's spine straightened with a shot of ice.

Natasha continued. "He was so sweet. We were hot and heavy for a few days. Then he hurt his knee, had a week off, and then he kind of pretended he didn't know me. So I brushed that off and moved on. Don't look at me like that. I know he's young. But he was so, so sweet. And besides, we only kissed. Hang on, I need a whizz."

She disappeared into the tiny bathroom, leaving Anya alone with the image of Will kissing Natasha. And then blanking her. Something cold and hard rose in her stomach, and for a second she thought she was going to be sick. Damn him. And damn her for falling for his kisses. Natasha was right, he *was* sweet. And she was stupid. *Stupid.*

A fizzing hit the back of her throat and she knew her body was telling her to cry. She refused. She was not going to cry over some boy band ass when she'd been through everything she had in the past couple of years. No fucking way. So she was being played? She could play him right back. At least she knew what was what now.

She pushed open the small curtain to her bunk and sat on the edge, looking through her bag for her toothbrush and toothpaste. She quickly changed into a tank and shorts, which was all she had to sleep in since the need for nightclothes didn't really occur on the street.

Natasha was taking her own sweet time in the bathroom, so she cleaned her teeth in the kitchen area and slid into bed. She pulled the curtain and switched on the little light. Out came the notebook again.

Kissed Natasha at the beginning of the tour

There. It was just a fact for a story. She sniffed and stuffed the book back in its hiding place. Nothing to worry about. Nothing to be upset about. Just a fact.

Chapter Eleven

As soon as the drivers pulled over for a bathroom break, Matt slipped out of his bunk. He hesitated for a second, wondering if he had time to make a recording of the snoring that was coming from one of the bunks, but decided that he had more important things to do.

He was on a mission.

He waited for all the drivers to congregate by the hut in the rest area. They called it a bathroom break, but it was more accurately a smoke break.

He slid out of the bus and found Hanging On. He pulled the manual handle on the outside of the bus and sneaked in. He should be a spy. Carefully closing the door, he wondered what his opening should be.

Come here often?

What's a nice place like you doing in a girl like this?

Maybe he should just kiss her awake. Except that felt a little…wrong.

Besides, he wanted her awake when he kissed her. Wanted to feel her lips meet his, her mouth open for him, her skin as he touched her neck—

Down boy.

There were only two bunks with the curtains closed. Shit. He hadn't thought this through. What if he woke up Natasha? He'd have to look for a clue. And then someone groaned and turned over, shoving a foot through the curtain. It had scarlet nails, which meant it wasn't Anya. Phew. God was clearly on his side.

He poked Anya through the curtain. Once, twice, and he was going to poke her a third time, but a hand flew out and grabbed his poking finger. It nearly gave him a heart attack.

"What are you doing?" she hissed at him, yanking as she pulled back the curtain.

"Learning that I would be the first to die in a horror movie. You scared the shit out of me." He unclenched his fists. Great. Now he looked like a wuss.

"How did you know it was me and not Natasha?" she asked with an accusing tone.

"Look. She shoved her hobbit foot out." He pointed at her bunk.

Anya slipped out of her bunk and stood in front of him. Shorter now that she didn't have shoes on, and oh my God, looking effing sexy in a long tank and shorts. He tried to keep his eyes on her face when all his hormones wanted him to do was look at her boobs.

Get a grip, Matt.

"She does not have a hobbit foot. That's just rude." She was all but tapping hers on the floor.

"Sorry. It was supposed to be funny. Come with me." He

pointed to the back of the bus and she frowned. To head off an objection, he turned and walked toward the rear. "Jesus. What's all this crap?" There were boxes and bags in front of the door that most people assumed was where the baggage was stored.

He shoved everything aside and opened the door. Instead of going down, steps went up. He climbed them, risking a tiny glance behind. Good, she was following. Clearly, she wasn't all sunshine when she'd just been woken up. That was okay. He had a feeling he'd also like grumpy Anya. Not that he was supposed to be liking her. He was supposed to be charming her to keep her distracted. Nothing more, nothing less.

Matt clicked on the light. The room at the top of the stairs wasn't exactly the same as the one in the band's bus. It was up a few stairs for one thing—the boys' just opened out on the same level. It also didn't have a drinks fridge, and the carpet was kind of a puke-inducing green swirl instead of the posh natural fiber carpet in theirs.

"Wow," Anya said as she emerged from the narrow stairway. Someone had let go of her grumps.

The room—although it was barely larger than a closet— had two chairs and one small sofa, but the real pull was the tinted rear window that stretched from the floor all the way over their head.

"This is nice. I can't believe I didn't know this was here."

She sat on the sofa, thank God, gazing out of the window at the night sky. She tucked her feet under her and settled her notebook in her lap. He sat next to her, but a respectful distance away. No sense in crowding her. "When did you pick up your notebook?" he asked.

"When you were chucking Natasha's boxes all over the place." She looked at him kind of weird, like he'd done something wrong, but he had no idea what. "Anyway, I have a bunch of questions for you that I haven't had the opportunity to ask yet. I figured this was a good time, since you woke me up quite rudely." She raised her nose at him, but was kind of smiling, too. Girls were so confusing.

"Ask me anything." He crossed his arms in front of him and sat back in the sofa, turning so he could see her.

She flipped through her notebook. "You don't seem at all shy to me. How did you get that nickname?"

"Which nickname? The Stud? That one?" He tried to use the diversion to straighten his answer in his head.

"The Shy Guy. How did you get that if you're really not that shy?" She cocked her head to one side, and all he could think about was angling his mouth over hers.

"Sorry, what? Oh yeah. Shy guy. Well that's the media for you. I am much shyer in front of lots of people, crowds, interviews…" He readjusted his posture so he could move an inch closer to her. "I'm just better one-on-one."

She obviously wasn't buying his charm. "You had an accident a month or so ago. What happened?"

Dammit. "It was a tragic synchronized dance accident," he deadpanned. "Very, very tragic."

She rolled her eyes, but her smile was more genuine than the one before. Shit. Was he really counting and grading her smiles?

"No really. What happened?"

He nodded in acceptance. "Okay. It was nothing. We were practicing the 'WET' number without the rubber floor. There was a rubber grid, but one of the bands was loose and my foot got stuck under it and I fell, twisting my knee. It pulled at my ACL, but the doctor said I could wait for surgery. So that's what I'm doing." He rubbed his right knee a little for effect.

"But I read a report saying that you'd *torn* your ACL and had to have emergency surgery in order to be able to make the tour. That wasn't right?" She took her pen out of the spiral on her book and removed the lid with her mouth. Her soft, sweet mouth. She stood up to look out of the window and all he could see was her long legs in those short shorts.

Get a grip, Matt.

"Media again. You can't trust them. Present company excepted."

She turned around and raised her eyebrows. Suddenly the bus lurched as it took off. Her eyes widened as she lost her balance and fell right at him. Instinctively, he reached out to steady her, but he half rose from the sofa and banged his head on the sloping ceiling. He fell back and took her with him.

"Ouch. Are you all right?" she asked, frowning.

Anya was in his lap, virtually astride him. Nothing would ever be better. He leaned in to her, wanting her to want to kiss him, too. She hesitated in a way she hadn't before. And then she kissed him. For a second it didn't feel right, and he was going to pull away and ask her what was wrong. But then she kind of sighed and kissed him like last time. Warm, intense, almost urgent. Heat rushed through him like adrenaline.

He gently moved her, so she wasn't pressing against his…lap, and drew away, running his fingers through her hair again and watching how it fell against her neck. "You're amazing."

She moved away a tiny bit and snorted a laugh again. "I bet you say that to all the girls."

"What girls? LJ keeps such a tight rein on us I haven't really seen a girl since I came on tour. Hey, maybe that's it. Maybe I'm so desperate for female company that I'm not as into you as I think I am." He smirked. That line had been pretty smooth.

But she sat way too upright.

What the hell…?

"No girls since you've been here, huh? I don't think that's the truth," she said. "But okay. If you want to play innocent…"

He frowned at that. What was she saying? "I never said I was innocent. I just said—"

"I know what you said."

He felt like he'd fallen down a rabbit hole. He pushed both hands through his hair and sat back. "Do you have any more questions for me?"

"Of course I do. Make yourself comfortable." She smiled naturally at that, and he relaxed a bit. "What's your favorite thing to do when you're not onstage?"

"I don't really know anymore. I can't remember what I used to like to do. Now I'm on tour, I like hanging with the guys, and we're all pretty masterful at World of Warcraft."

"What if you were on a date? What's your favorite first date thing to do?" She was still scribbling down World of Warcraft and he could see that she'd put a question mark next to it in her notes. Weird.

"First date stuff, huh? Is this on or off the record?" He grinned.

"Everything you've ever said to me is on the record. Why would you think we were ever off the record?"

His smile faltered as he tried to remember things he'd said to her. He'd been pretty careful, he thought. Oh well, if he kept her on-side, maybe she wouldn't file her story until Will came back. Then he could deal with her.

A pang of regret pierced his stomach, and in a second, he realized he would effing kill his brother if he laid a hand on Anya. And that made zero sense, because Matt couldn't have her, either. How would that work out?

"What's wrong?" she asked. "You're looking like a deer caught in headlights." She slipped farther away, sitting on the arm of the sofa with her feet on the cushion.

"What? Nothing. First date, huh?" He got up, careful to avoid the curved fiberglass part of the ceiling, and stretched, placing his hands flat on the glass window above them. "I guess I would pick her up in the afternoon, maybe take her out for coffee or an iced tea. Then we'd go for a walk, and after a few minutes I'd take her hand, see if she liked it or not. Then if she seemed to like it, I might try to put my arm around her." He closed his eyes and imagined an actual first date with Anya. "If she didn't pull away, it would only be a matter of time before I…took her to dinner. And then maybe on the walk home, I might kiss her. If she let me."

Silence.

• • •

Anya knew she was gawking, but she couldn't help it. His low, hypnotic voice made her think that she was the one on the date with him. She was the one he was kissing. Her pen was poised on the pad, but she just stared at him talking with his eyes closed.

She jumped a mile when he caught her staring. He didn't move, but his eyes half closed. He reached out his arm to her. "Come here, angel."

How dare he? She was just another girl to him…another Natasha, another…who knew who. She tried to vibe outrage, but her body betrayed her as she crawled over to him and let him wrap his arm around her, pulling her head against his chest. Safe. Not alone. She held in even the hint of tears. She wouldn't cry.

He was so big and strong, and she did feel unbelievably safe with him. She felt his heartbeat under her ear. Her hand stretched out over his chest, hesitantly feeling the heat beneath her fingers. She breathed when he did and relaxed as he stroked her back. Maybe she could just enjoy this while he liked her. Until he Natasha'd her.

What was she doing here? She hated that the stupid one hundred dollar per diem had erased some of her hunger for the scoop. She still hadn't found a whiff. Except for Alice Singleton and Natasha. She wondered what Alice looked like. Natasha and Anya couldn't be more different both physically and…well, age-wise for one thing. Yet here she was, and nothing in her would let her move away from him. Not one cell urged her to leave.

His hand slid under her tank at the back. She tensed for a second, and he stopped moving. It was such an intimate touch, but no, she didn't want to do anything that would take his skin away from hers.

She relaxed again, and he continued stroking her. It was nothing. Nothing compared to what she'd seen people do on the streets when they thought no one was looking.

His hand stayed on the small of her back, just slowly stroking, stroking, until his proximity, his bare hand against her bare skin made her feel as if she was on the slow chug up a rollercoaster. She could hear the blood pumping around her body as she waited for the plunge down to the ground.

Suddenly she didn't care who he was and what she was doing here. Her whole body was telling her that she wanted to touch him the way he was touching her. For him to feel what she was feeling now. The silence between them only served to enhance every emotion, thought, and sensation that ran through her.

She sat up without saying anything. His eyes followed her as she stood, hesitating for a moment as if her body was complaining about being away from his, then she placed one hand on his shoulder and deliberately placed one knee either side of his lap. His thighs were as hard as his chest. Heat pumped through her again. She took a deep breath. "It seems…all I can think about is kissing you."

"Jesus," he whispered.

"No. It's Anya," she whispered right back. Why was he so compelling? Why was she so weak like this with him? She felt like a totally different person. Could this be her? The real her that she'd been hiding for years? Or was this some whole other Anya?

He grabbed a handful of her hair and gently tugged her toward him. "No one's ever said that to me before." His gaze was on her mouth.

"What? That they want to kiss you?" She was being pulled closer and closer.

"Mmm-hmm," was all he said before his lips touched

hers.

She opened her mouth for him, but he pulled away slightly, gently stroking his bottom lip against hers. She could feel his breath in her mouth, and it felt like he was living inside her as she inhaled. Her whole body felt like it was vibrating in anticipation of his kiss.

As he yanked her whole body to his, his mouth crushed against hers, sending a zip of electricity up her spine. She couldn't help but moan as he devoured her. Both his hands dived up the back of her tank top and she pressed against them, wanting to feel his skin.

Suddenly he tore his lips from hers and held her at arms' length. "I'm sorry. I can't do this. I don't have anything with me."

"Anything...? What do you mean?"

"I don't have any condoms. I never expected..."

She leaped back, off his lap and onto the floor, trying to ease up on the heavy breathing that was wracking her body. "What? What? No!"

He snatched a cushion from the sofa and shoved it on his lap, looking at her in confusion.

Oh. *Ohhhh.* "I'm sorry. I didn't mean..." she started to say.

"Oh my God, no. That was really presumptuous wasn't it? I'm sorry. I jumped like five hurdles at once." He looked really embarrassed, and she wondered if her face was as red as his.

She took a breath and sat on the floor cross-legged in front of him, not touching him at all, until she leaned forward and rested the very top of her head against his knee.

"I'm sorry. I got totally carried away by how lush you are. I've never..."

"Lush?" she raised her head.

"I've been hanging out with Miles too much. His British-isms are rubbing off on me." He grinned and flopped back against the sofa, taking a deep breath. "Anyway, what I'm trying to say is 'my bad.'"

She felt like saying something truly honest. "You make me feel different. I mean I've never felt the way I feel when I'm kissing you. But I've never…done *that* before."

"It's okay, neither have I," he said with a smile.

"Is that a lie?" She knew it was and grinned back at him.

"Pretty much, but I didn't want you to feel alone."

They sat in silence for a few seconds, just looking at each other. Then Will cleared his throat and pulled the sofa cushion more on to his lap.

Anya looked blankly at him for a second and then collapsed back on the floor giggling.

His matching laugh was warm and genuine. She lay there looking up at the sky, with her bare feet now on top of his, watching as the stars and clouds zoomed by.

Could this be any more perfect?

Chapter Twelve

The next day was a rush of auditing. Something the band had to do whenever they reached a new venue. Each of the band members was responsible for making sure all their own costumes were present and accounted for backstage, that their guest lists were up to date, that they knew where the stage entrances and exits were, where all the cabling lay, what kind of floor the stage had.

It was a day spent almost entirely with the other guys, going over steps and set lists. Ryder had had to go to the doctor with a sore throat and swollen glands, so they were sitting on the stage watching for his arrival to make sure he could sing that night.

Matt found himself watching for Anya, too. Looking for a flash of her shiny hair, or the sound of her clomping boots. Nada. He hoped he hadn't fucked it up the night before. He'd never, ever felt so into a girl before. Like he wanted to pull her apart, see who she was inside, and then put her back

together again. He was painfully aware that he was beginning to sound like a creepy serial killer in his own head. Not
that there were many un-creepy serial killers.

"What do you think, Will?"

He snapped out of his daydream. "What?"

"If Ryder's not able to sing, can you take the lead on
'Hanging On'?" Trevin asked from his vantage point, sitting
on one of the big black amps in front of the drum set.

"I guess." Shit, he'd have to spend the day practicing.
Which meant he couldn't go find Anya. "Will I get a run-
through before the show?"

"You wuss—what do you need a run-through for?"
Ryder stepped onto the stage from the wings. "Anyway, I'm
fine. Just have to gargle and spray some kind of salty fluid
at the back of my throat." He held up a large bottle with a
prescription label.

All of them laughed except for Nathan who looked be-
mused. "Don't worry, Nath. You'll understand when you're
older, mate," Miles said, giving the poor guy a noogie.

"So what's up with you and that reporter chick?" Trevin
asked in such a way that Matt knew it had a double meaning.

"I've got her under control. Don't worry."

"Her?" Miles swiveled around and raised his sunglasses.
"You have 'her' under control? How does that work?"

"I meant 'it'. I have 'it' under control." He couldn't possibly have Anya less under control. Under his skin, yeah. The
rest? Not so much.

"Just be charming. And don't chuck any of us under the
bus. Ix nay on our secrets," Miles said.

"I don't have any secrets," Nathan said, shrugging.

Lucky bastard.

Trevin stood up. "Okay, I guess that's us for this afternoon. Nathan, I think you're up first for makeup today, but check the list on the door just in case."

Matt made a run for the edge of the stage and jumped down.

"Your knee really seems to be better," called LJ from the third row of seats. Where had he come from? "Amazing recovery, really." His face was static. No emotion. No happiness at his recovery. Shit. Did he really suspect?

Matt hesitated for a moment and then continued walking. "Thanks to you," he said as he rushed past the man who had put his brother in rehab.

Don't let me hit him. Don't let me hit him.

He repeated his mantra until he was out of the seating area and back to the bus.

He checked the makeup list as he went in and, indeed, it was Nathan up first, followed by him. Pulling his phone out of his pocket he sat heavily in one of the booths. He checked Instagram, then his private Twitter account, and then he couldn't help but go to WowSounds.com.

On the Road

Thank you for all the great comments, I'm going to start reading some of them to Will, see if he feels like replying to any of them. Put your lippy on, ladies, he might be looking at YOU(r) comment.

It turns out the post-show euphoria lasts a long time. A loooong time. If you were one of the last out of the stadium last night, the chances are that Will was watching you leave from his perch on the roof.

Boy seems to like heights, or the sky, and he can even name some stars (not counting Nathan, Ryder, Miles, and Trevin).

Matt grinned and made a mental note to Google some star names to identify for her next time.

If you're a World of Warcraft girl, you are already on Will's list. He's an expert at the game, as it seems are the rest of the band. They play online under aliases, so who knows? You could have already played them!

And in the best news of the day, I've been told to take photos…so look out for some candid photos of the not-so-shy guy, Will. What will I catch him doing? What would you LIKE me to catch him doing? Keep it clean please!

More from NOLA tomorrow! Stay tuned to WowSounds.com!

Photos? Maybe she'd let him take photos of her, too? He wished he already had one to look at. That's it. This evening's mission is to get photos. This evening. Hmmm. He knew a couple of the guys were breaking out to go see Bourbon Street in the French Quarter. Maybe he'd take Anya, too. It would be good to get out. It was so busy down there Ryder had assured them that with minimal disguise they'd have a great time.

Or maybe he'd just keep her to himself.

• • •

It was so weird. There was even a photo of him online with bandages around his knee. She flipped through the pages of the fan site. She couldn't help but marvel at the fact that she was actually kissing the guy who was in so many photos and magazines. It was strange. When they were together, he didn't feel famous. But when they were apart, she couldn't put together the Will in the photos and the Will she knew. Kissed. Whatever. It was like two different Wills.

She grabbed her notebook and paged back nearly to the beginning. Will had been brought up in Jacksonville, Florida, and she knew somewhere she'd written down the name of his high school. There it was: Joseph Hood Memorial High School.

She underlined it slowly. Should she? No. That's, like, totally stalkerish. This was a tour thing. Given what Natasha had said, it could just be a couple of days thing. She shouldn't be mooning. She shouldn't be wanting to see what Alice Singleton looked like. Who would ever find out? She quickly searched for his school online and clicked through their gallery by year.

Okay, she could stop now. But she didn't want to. She clicked on the right year for his ninth grade and scanned the names attributed to some of the candid shots. Singleton, Singleton, Singleton. *There*!

She was really sweet looking, all straight blond hair pulled back with an Alice band. Appropriate. She looked a bit like Natasha—all fine features and really pale skin.

Nothing like Anya.

She turned to her Will page and wrote more facts.

Twisted his right knee.

Says he hasn't kissed anyone on the tour. (lie)

Definitely kisses on the first date. (see Natasha)

Has had sex before. Wonder who with?

She shook her head and snapped out of it, closing down the school site and tapping her fingers on the table. Her email blinked and she opened that instead.

Mrs. Anderson.

Please make yourself available to meet me Thursday at the Rendezvous Café in the French Quarter. It would be great to see you there at, say, 1:00 p.m.? Let me know if that suits you. I'll bring your checks and we can discuss how long you'll be staying with the tour and how long your children and husband can cope without you!

Best wishes,

Cynthia

Stress peppered her shoulders, pulling her muscles tighter and tighter. She hunched them to try and ease the stiffening. No, no, no. No. One look at Anya and Cynthia would know full well that she wasn't a married woman with kids. Her job would be over, and she'd probably have her pass revoked. Probably? Definitely. Today might be the last day with Will. Her last chance to get her scoop. Her last chance to spend every second kissing him that she could. A cold infiltrated her stomach and she wrapped both arms around her middle.

A granola bar hit the top of her head. "Eat," Natasha said. "You look super pale. Are you okay?"

"Sure, I'm fine," Anya pushed out weakly.

"And I'm Beyonce. Wanna see me shake ma thang?" She turned around, hitched her shirt up, and shook her ass at what seemed like a hundred miles an hour.

Anya laughed, there was no way she couldn't. "How's Nick?"

"Nice sidestep, girl. What's up?" She slipped into the

opposite seat and leaned forward. "I'm all ears."

"Really it's nothing." Anya started to pick at her cuticles which, even as she did it, she knew was one hell of a tell. She looked up and stuffed her hands underneath her thighs.

"Is it Will?" Natasha asked. "I don't mean to intrude, but I heard you talking last night in the back room. I had no idea you were in any way close...or I wouldn't have mentioned... you know." She cocked her head in sympathy.

"Oh God," Anya moaned and put her head on the table.

"Come on. It's okay. Tell Aunty Tasha about it. I'm older and wiser."

She picked up her head. "You mean you're faking being older."

"Oh sweetie. Whatever you say, at twenty-three I'm still a lot older than you, aren't I?"

Anya couldn't say anything. Everything seemed to be imploding around her.

"Okay, enough. I have an hour before I see Nathan for makeup. Let's bust this joint and go find some coffee. We can talk. Really. I'm a great friend if you give me a chance." Her voice was soft, and the expression in her eyes couldn't have been more genuine.

Maybe she needed a friend. Natasha had assured her that they were friends now. Family even, and she really hadn't done anything to make Anya think Natasha *wouldn't* be a friend. But she'd lived so long depending on just herself and Jude. And she never really spoke to Jude. Even when he was there physically for her, he had rarely been there mentally. She wanted—needed—to take a leap of faith. She nodded and stood, hoping she wasn't about to make the biggest mistake of her life.

A few minutes later she was spilling. Partially, at least. There was no sense in boring Natasha with all her pathetic life issues, but she did explain about meeting her boss at WowSounds and that she thought Anya was married with kids. When she'd finished, Natasha just looked at her, mouth open, eyes round. She goggled Anya for a good ten seconds.

And then she laughed. Firstly a huff almost of disbelief. Then what can only be described as a guffaw, and then she was giggling, holding on to the table in the snack hut. Like, literally holding on.

Anya was stunned. And then she saw a sliver of desperate humor. In an "if you didn't laugh you'd cry" way. She cracked a smile. And then she was laughing, too. More at the snot running down Natasha's face and her seeming inability to sit up straight in her chair.

"Oh God, I'm sorry. I'm not laughing at you. Just… What a fix to get yourself into." She shook her head. "Are you going to meet her?"

"I don't know. I guess I can't claim twenty-four hour rabies, can I? Can I?" Could she?

"Is that a thing? It could be I guess," Natasha said. "So the bottom line is, you have to see her and pretend to be, say…twenty-four? That's probably the youngest you'd be able to fake claiming a hubby and kids."

"I don't even have anything to wear that would be right for someone that old." She mentally scanned the clothes she had and it took about 0.3 seconds.

"Come find me before you go to meet her, I'll see if I can't put together a look that might see you through. And if I can't, I'll go for you. I've read all your blogs, so I know what she'll be expecting. Don't worry about it. See? Aunty

Tasha can fix everything! Oh my God, I just realized: if you get fired you won't be back here again, will you? No more Will, no more articles…shit, that blows. I'm definitely going to come up with something, okay?"

"Okay," she almost whispered. Natasha was right—no more Will. She couldn't get her head around that one. Nor her heart. She had to do anything she could to stay. She… she was doing this for Jude, right? Was it wrong of her to be thinking about losing Will, too?

Natasha hugged her awkwardly over the table, and Anya had no words to express the emotion that was bubbling up in her chest. Someone wanted to look out for her. Someone was willing to help her. It was unfathomable. The last month her mother had been coherent, all she'd said was that everybody was out to get them, and that Anya shouldn't trust anyone, rely on anyone. To be honest, she'd kind of taken the advice to heart, except where Jude was concerned. She released Natasha and sat back down. "Thank you so much."

"You're welcome, honey."

They fell silent for a minute or so while they sipped their coffees. And then the door burst open and banged against the side of the hut so hard that the whole place shook. Natasha rolled her eyes at Anya and whispered, "Sister Act," out of the corner of her mouth.

"What did you say?" the older of the two girls demanded. She was tall, immaculately made-up, even though she didn't look old enough to need that much camouflage. She dug her fists into her waist, eyes flashing.

The younger girl with her slunk away, head down, toward the woman who was making the coffee.

Natasha grinned. "I didn't say anything to you, sugah,"

she drawled.

"I can get you fired in a heartbeat, so watch it." Wow, she was so…*nasty*.

"And how many people have you said that to this afternoon, sugah? Ten? Twenty? It kind of loses effect when that's the only thing you have to say. Why don't you try being nice to people for a change?"

"I don't need to be nice. I'm famous," she sneered back. Anya guessed she had a point there.

"Why don't you go terrorize someone who cares? We're done here." Natasha rose from the table and Anya hurried to follow. She did *not* want to be left here with Cruella de Vil.

Outside, Anya couldn't help but say something. "I don't think I've ever seen anyone be so mean to people in real life."

Natasha sighed. "Yeah, I know. Someone should tell her that life isn't actually like some show on the CW. But it ain't gonna be me. I need my job. And this is a *great* job."

"Thank you again for helping me," Anya said as they started walking back to the parking lot full of trailers and buses.

"You're welcome. It's nice to have you around, honestly. Maybe I'm being selfish by helping you."

She squeezed Anya's arm, and tears threatened to well up in her eyes. People were nice. Well, maybe except Cruella. Maybe there were other people out there who would help her, too. Maybe she didn't need to live her life all alone, all the time. She would think about that.

"Hey, stop by the makeup trailer in about an hour. I should be doing Will then." She shook her head. "Not *doing* him. You know…just doing his makeup."

Anya couldn't help but laugh at her sudden concern. "It's okay. I knew what you meant. Okay, I'll drop by."

"I think you'll like it. The makeup chair is like a confessional. Let's see what we can get him to spill for your blog posts. I love them, by the way." She winked and left Anya in front of Hanging On.

Chapter Thirteen

It was pretty crappy going into makeup second. Not as bad as first, of course, but that extra forty-five minutes or so didn't give you really enough time to do anything except constantly check the time to make sure you weren't late. Makeup going long because you were late did not endear you to the other guys. He'd already fucked that up once since he joined the band, and the show that night had been hell.

But then again, he didn't want to be too early, because Natasha had always acted a little weird toward him. At five minutes to his showtime he went into the makeup trailer.

Nathan was still in the chair chatting to Natasha and… Anya. A flush of attraction flicked through him, and he sucked in his stomach instinctively. But then he realized she'd be watching him put on makeup. Shit. There was nothing whatsoever sexy about watching a guy get made up, he was sure of it.

"Sorry, Will. We're running a bit behind." Before he

could glare at Nathan, she continued. "It was my bad. I couldn't find my last tube of Watertight Base, so I had to run to my trailer and find the new shipment."

Heat rose in his face, he could feel it. He'd taken the semi-used makeup the night of the previous show. He was still hiding a lot…

He ducked his head and sat on the other side of the trailer from Anya. He hoped he wasn't actually blushing, although, thankfully, the light in the trailer was horrible except for the corner in which Natasha worked. That was ablaze with lights. All the better to see their imperfections.

He looked up at Anya and smiled. She blushed. Great. They were both embarrassed.

"Did LJ give you hassle when you left the stage? I heard him say something to you as you left," Nathan said from the chair.

Anya's head snapped up. She probably thought it was about her.

"He's a joy to be around, I'll give you that," Matt non-answered. He shifted in his seat and tried to get a read on her face. Was she embarrassed about last night? About what they did? Their making-out? It had been really intense. He decided to act. To force her hand in front of Natasha and Nathan.

He stood up and slid into the booth next to her and draped his arm around her. *Take that, awkwardness.* In that second, he realized this was more than just charming Anya. He wanted more than that from her, wanted to know more about her. No, he wanted to know everything.

Both Nathan and Natasha froze for a split second, watching his reflection in the mirror. So he guessed their secret was out. Well, too bad. He didn't want it to be a secret. Anya stiffened for a second, and then leaned against him and put her hand on his thigh. Right. Everything was still cool, then. "You going to watch the show tonight?" he asked her.

She hesitated. "It…depends on how many dares I have left."

Matt laughed. "I can't believe I didn't use more of those last night." He squeezed her shoulder. "You've only worked off one, so you have four left. And yes, before you ask, I'm adding more. So yes. You still have to dance."

"Natasha?" she called. "Are you watching the show tonight?"

"Sure am, sweetie. I rarely miss 'em," she replied from her corner.

"Can I go with you?"

"Of course you can! Who else can I make fun of Sister Act with?"

"Sister Act?" Nathan asked.

"I mean Cherry."

"Ouch. Do not let Paige hear you say that. She has *not* been in a good mood recently," Nathan said.

Natasha laughed. "Sweetheart. When has she *ever* been in a good mood?"

"Well, when she was hooking up with Miles, she was pretty damn happy." Nathan shrugged.

"That's only because she was planning world domination and babies and things," Natasha retorted. "You all know that."

"True," Nathan said. "Good thing he saw through her before he fell in love with her. I think she had this weird idea that because Miles is English, she would somehow become royalty if she married him. Do you remember, Will? She started wearing those tiaras everywhere, not just onstage."

Matt started. "I don't remember." He couldn't concentrate on anything except the swirls Anya's fingertips were making on his leg.

Nathan said, "What do you mean you can't remember? You made fun of her to her face about becoming Queen of England and asking her how many ladies-in-waiting she'd have. I didn't even know what ladies-in-waiting were, remember? You told me to watch *The Tudors*. I did, and my mom nearly killed me." He grinned wickedly. "So now I just watch it on my phone."

"What's *The Tudors*?" Anya asked.

"You've never heard of *The Tudors*? It was a series about Henry the Eighth of England and his six lovely wives," Matt said.

"So why was your mom upset at you for watching it? It sounds educational," she asked Nathan.

"Riiiiight. You can take that one, Will," Nathan said between clenched teeth as Natasha put that weird tan pencil stuff around the outside of his lips.

"It was less educational and more…what's the word I'm looking for?" Matt said.

"Porny? Is that the word you were looking for?" Natasha piped in.

"Maybe a little porny…but educationy, too. I swear," Matt said. One look at Nathan's face in the mirror and he started laughing. Nathan had to push Natasha's hand away so he could laugh without her drawing all over his face.

Natasha whacked him on the shoulder. "Keep still you

little perv, or none of you will make the show on time!" She shoved a tissue in his hand, and he wiped away the tears of laughter that were messing with his makeup.

Matt turned to Anya. "Okay, before I get this done, you have to promise that you won't be grossed out by me with makeup on." He held out his little finger. "Pinky swear?"

She grabbed his finger with hers. "Pinky swear. Actually I think it's really…attracti—interesting, I mean. Very *Cabaret*."

"What's *Cabaret*?" he asked, although a good three quarters of his brain was echoing with the word "attractive."

"Hang on a sec. Look." She pulled up some YouTube clips of this hot woman dancing in a smoky club, and a man with a shit ton of eye makeup on. It was kind of elegantly sleazy. It *was* kind of attractive. In a dark way.

"How do you know that? Who is that girl?" he asked.

"It was a movie from way back. Like old even when my mom used to watch it. The girl is Liza Minnelli. She's awesome in the movie."

"Maybe we can watch it tonight after the show. I bet we can find it on Netflix."

She frowned like he was saying words she didn't understand, but still agreed. "Sure. If you think you can sit still after the show."

Before he could answer, Natasha brushed off Nathan, sent him to wardrobe, and spun the chair around for Matt. "My lord," she said, flicking the seat with a small towel.

He rolled his eyes at her and sat down. She clipped his hair away from his face and wiped lotion on his skin with a cotton ball.

"So I see you've been hospitable to Anya since she got here. That's mighty gentlemanly of you," she said in her southern accent.

"I am nothing but a gentleman." He grinned in the mirror at Anya. At least she couldn't argue that. But he saw both their faces fall a little. Anya's eyes flicked to Natasha and back to her tablet. "What? What did I do?"

There was a small silence before Natasha said, "Nothing, sugah. Nothing at all."

"He's been very gentlemanly to me, I promise," Anya said.

"Well that's all right then." Silence.

"What have you been up to?" Matt asked Natasha.

"LJ asked me to come on the world tour a few weeks ago, so I've been trying to rearrange all my other jobs so I can come with you guys."

"Oh, I didn't know you were heading off on a world tour. I probably should have known that, shouldn't I? Where are you going?" Anya asked.

Matt looked at Natasha to answer, as she looked at him to answer. Except he couldn't. He'd paid exactly zero attention to the world tour plans because he knew he wouldn't be going. Will would be back by then. "Europe?" he guessed.

She rolled her eyes as she applied what she called "primer." "It's mainly a European tour, but because we're also going to Japan for a record ten shows, they can officially call it a world tour. I've also heard rumors of Australia, which will be cool."

"Sounds exciting," Anya said.

"I'm excited," Natasha said. "I've got a contact to hook me up with a woman who does traditional geisha makeup, and she said she'd show me how to do it. I'm saving up so I can buy the genuine supplies there."

"That's cool," Anya said. He wondered if she was thinking about how they would continue their relationship. He wished he could say, "Don't worry, I'll be starting college in the fall." But he couldn't. Couldn't reassure her. Didn't even know if she needed reassurance.

"Yup," Matt agreed, although he wasn't sure what geisha makeup was.

Natasha's fingers pattered lightly across his face. "It's funny. Since you had your accident…" Her voice trailed off, and Anya's head snapped up in the mirror.

What's that about?

"Since my accident, what?" He frowned.

Natasha paused and then shrugged. "You must have face planted really hard, because since you came back, your bone structure is different. Not hugely, but just a fraction of an inch here and there. It's weird. I never thought a bad fall could shift things around like that, but they obviously can." She pulled out a huge fluffy brush for powder. "Hold your breath."

He waited for the cloud of powder to settle and wondered what to say. At least she had somehow provided her own excuse for how different his bone structure was from his brother's.

"So what you're saying is that I'm more ruggedly handsome than I was before?"

Before she could answer, his phone rang. He looked at the display. It was Mom.

He swiped his finger across the screen and held up a finger to Natasha, who nodded and left him alone and went to arrange her brushes.

"Hey, Mom," he said, ducking into the bathroom.

"How's it going there, darling?"

"So far so good. How're…things there?"

"I have great news. He's finished rehab. Just turned a corner and is really healthy now. He thinks he can join the tour again."

Matt's heart started beating fast. He peeked out at Anya chatting to Natasha. "So soon? Are you sure that's a good idea?" He winced at himself. He was letting his feelings for Anya overshadow everything.

"I'm fairly sure. This is great news, Matt. It means you can come back to *your* life. Aren't you happy?"

"I am. It is awesome news. Thump him for me, will ya?"

"He'll be in touch soon with a plan for the switch, okay?"

"Okay."

"Break a leg tonight."

"Thanks. Love you."

"Love you too, darling." She hung up.

He gazed again at Anya in the mirror, cold trickling through him. He had just a matter of days with her, and then he had to disappear, leaving her to think she was in a relationship with Will.

He'd started off wanting to have a bit of fun with her. But he'd gone beyond that. He'd fallen for her. He'd kissed her. And in the end, he would have no choice but to abandon her. Or try to. The thought of Will taking up where Matt had left off turned his stomach.

Probably shoulda thought this one through better.

• • •

So all Anya had learned was that boys will be boys, even

the cute ones who you think definitely wouldn't be watching *The Tudors* on their phone. Not sure how she could weave that into her story, and even if she could, did she really want to get Nathan into trouble with his mom?

She just wasn't cut out for this. Her homeless piece had been close to her heart, and no one was hurt by her writing it. But finding a scoop for money? Screwing people over? People that she knew? It just felt all kinds of wrong.

Her ruthless bone had disappeared the second she stepped foot into the plush bus she was currently calling home. Not that she really knew any of them, even Will, who seemed to always be just slightly off. When he was onstage, he was the most confident person in the world. But as soon as he was offstage, he became hesitant, almost like he was second guessing everything he said or did. Until he relaxed, and then it was virtually impossible to imagine he'd ever been shy.

Almost like he were two people.

But that kind of thing only happened in the movies. Besides, he knew she was here to get some dirt on him. Who wouldn't be nervous?

But she still couldn't see herself humiliating someone in public. Not for fun, or for money. It was wrong, and she didn't want to ever be the person who did that.

After Will had headed off to costume, Natasha had told her to come back when her last makeup of the evening—Ryder—had left. When she returned, Natasha was screwing tops back on tubes and organizing everything

"Sit down. It's your turn now," she said, grinning.

"What? No, no it's okay, don't worry." She didn't want her to go to any trouble when she'd offered to help her the following day.

"It's no trouble. In fact it'll help for tomorrow. I can get a feel for your skin and the colors that suit you. Sit." She spun the chair around and pointed at the seat.

"Yes, ma'am."

"I want you to look magical tonight. It's a sultry night, and you and I are going to make the most of it." She grabbed some bottles and cotton balls and got to work.

"What do you mean sultry?" Anya asked.

"It's hot, and humid, and adventure is beckoning. Don't you feel it? We have backstage passes for the biggest band in the world right now, we're in the mix. And we have the best seats in the house. Doesn't that get your blood rushing? It does for me. Maybe New Orleans is my spiritual home, but there's just something in the air."

"Okaaay," Anya drawled, but in truth she did feel it. But it wasn't New Orleans. She realized she was watching history being made here. Maybe not world-altering history, but something important all the same. And Natasha's enthusiasm was infectious.

"Tell me something about you that no one else knows." Natasha said, her mouth half closed around the end of a makeup brush.

Anya half laughed. "That's easy. No one knows anything about me!" Why did she say that? But even as she said the words—the truth—a tiny beam of light played with her soul. *Maybe the truth does set you free*?

Natasha took out the brush. "What do you mean?"

She tried for a little more light. "My mom left me alone in our house when I was fifteen. I've been on my own since then." A little lighter. Was sharing her secrets the answer?

Natasha hadn't hesitated in sympathizing with her about the meeting with her boss, maybe she was the right person to speak to. Even making the decision to tell her made the load she was carrying seem pounds lighter.

"What? Sweetie. What happened to you? Where do you live now?" Natasha squatted down in front of her, concern etched over her somewhat sparkly face.

"I live in Hanging On right now. My backpack holds everything I own. I have to meet my boss tomorrow, and she thinks I'm like twenty-seven with kids and a husband. When she sees me, she'll know I'm none of those things. And if I lose my job tomorrow, I'll have to hitch back to Tulsa and maybe find a shelter to stay in."

"My ever-living God. What? No, no, no. I'm not going to let that happen. If you get fired we'll figure something out, okay? You poor, poor girl. How old are you really?"

Anya hiccoughed. "Seventeen." Tears trickled down her face of their own accord. How could one random person, one solitary person who cared, save her life by offering help?

Natasha wrapped her arms around her, stroking her hair. "You poor, poor soul. You're so brave. I'm going to look after you now, okay? I'm going to make you up tomorrow, and you'll nail this meeting with your boss, and you can stay with us for the rest of the tour. We'll be our own Sister Act." She shook her head. "I don't know how you've survived. But I'm glad you did. We'll figure everything out together.

"Now stop crying, or I'm not going be able to make you look spectacular tonight."

Anya laughed with a freedom that made her lightheaded. "Thank you, Natasha. For being so nice."

"You're welcome," she replied simply. "You see. They

don't call the makeup seat 'the confessional' for nothing. It works every time." She smiled at her in the mirror.

Anya felt free for the first time in about five years. In truth, she'd been looking after her mother for years before she actually left. She hadn't realized how heavily it had laid around her, inside her. Pressing her down, making her feel tight and on edge. A lot of that had disappeared.

She watched Natasha work in the mirror. How could someone be so open to helping a virtual stranger? Father Howard did, but he was all religious, and he *had* to be kind like that. And Jude. He had been in her same position. But no one else, literally no one, had ever offered her help or support before Natasha. Were there more people out there like that? The idea had never really crossed her mind. Surely if there were, there wouldn't be any homelessness?

But then...what about Will? Could she tell him?

She wanted to—so badly—but what if he didn't want to know a fake reporter with no home? What if he treated her like he treated Natasha? Just pretending there was nothing between them. Or got her fired, or broke her heart.

She closed her eyes for a second, feeling the heartbreak that was just over the horizon. No. No. She couldn't risk telling him. It was too dangerous. Too...everything.

Natasha was one thing. Will was something totally different.

She opened her eyes, resolute. "You won't tell anyone, will you?" She hated how pathetic her voice sounded.

Natasha frowned. "No, sugar. Not a soul. To my deathbed, okay?"

"Thank you," she said, relieved.

"I'm going to curl your hair, too, okay? It'll look so lovely down for once."

"Okay." She remembered how Will had liked it down.

Using her curling iron, Natasha made her shoulder-length hair look shorter, with waves and curls looking like she'd just got out of bed. But with a full face of makeup, it looked wild and exciting. Natasha took a soft brush and dipped it in some really fine glitter and painted it delicately on some ends of her hair. She sprayed it lightly and stood back to admire her work.

"Stunning. If I say so myself."

Anya looked at herself. "Ditto, and ditto. You're a miracle worker."

"Nah. I had a great canvas to work with. But now we have to find you something to wear. Stay here." She ran out of the trailer, leaving her spinning from one side to the other, watching the glitter flash at the ends of her curls.

When Natasha came back, she was holding a gold, shimmering sundress. "Here. I found a loaner. It's going to be perfect with your coloring."

"Who does it belong to? I'm guessing no one in the band!"

"Ha! You might be surprised. No, kidding. It was one of Paige's costumes that didn't make the cut. She hated it and refused to wear it. So it just hangs in the costume trailer. We'll put it back tomorrow. We use her rejected dresses all the time. She likes tight, low-cut things, and the first costume designer had brought outfits that were age-appropriate for her, but she wanted to look older. Go try it on." She pointed toward the bathroom.

It was made of some kind of brocade, a slightly stiff material, which helped keep it up, as it was off the shoulder in a slightly old-fashioned way. It was a lighter gold color than she had first thought. The neckline went across her chest and around her upper arms. It fell from the fitted waist to her knees. She closed her eyes, trying for a second to lock in the memory of her in the dress. It was perfect. And Will would love her in it. Hell, *she* loved her in it!

And because it was designed like a sundress, she could wear her plain, black flip-flops with it without it looking too odd. She emerged from the bathroom, her jean skirt and T-shirt in her hand.

"God, I'm brilliant." Natasha whispered when she came out. She jumped up and pumped her fist in the air. "Seriously. I'm effing amazing! You look crazy good!"

She grabbed a hangered dress, covered in a dry cleaning bag, out of the kitchen. "My turn. I'll be right back."

She came back nearly immediately in a figure-hugging, black sleeveless dress with large red flowers patterned across the middle that kind of made her waist look tiny. "Wow. That's a great dress."

"Thanks, sweetie. You ready to hit the show?" She pulled on some impossibly high sandals and planted her fists on her hips. "We are going to have an awesome night if I have to kill someone to achieve it. Okay?"

"Okay. But let's hope it doesn't come to that."

"Let's hit it, sister!"

Anya was aware of the looks they both got on the short walk to the stadium. Roadies and backstage people, who hadn't ever looked at her twice before, suddenly couldn't take their eyes off them. Maybe it was just Natasha. She looked like she just stepped off the front page of a magazine.

"Uh-oh. Badly timed," Natasha said, slowing down. Across the parking lot, the girl who had been so mean to them in the coffee hut was stalking toward her trailer, a bunch of people in tow. Just as Anya looked at her, Paige caught their eyes and glared at them. And then smirked. Maybe it was a smile? Whatever it was sent a little shiver down Anya's spine.

"It's like locking eyes with a shark," Natasha mumbled, exaggerating a shiver. "Okay. Eyes on the prize." She seemed to know her way through the new stadium, although Anya probably could have followed the noise, too.

The podium was fairly empty this time. Probably not as many guests the first night in town. Natasha said hello to two girls and hugged them both briefly, but as she seemed about to introduce Anya, the band started up. Natasha shrugged, and everyone smiled and nodded at one another.

Natasha *had* been right. There was definitely something exciting in the air tonight. The thumping bass shuddered through her already lightened body. She wanted to dance and shout, scream and leap around like a kid before Christmas. A *normal* kid before Christmas.

The music was as infectious as before, even though they played a slightly different set. Through the stage cutouts she could see the audience, with neon bands around their heads and wrists, jumping and holding their arms out to the boys. She couldn't believe she was actually a part of this. How many of those girls would kill to be where she was now?

Maybe this gig was going to save her. Not by writing a scoop, but by meeting nice people and having one of them, maybe two of them, actually care about her. Maybe that's all it would take to help her get off the street.

She took a few photos with her tablet, until Natasha grabbed it and took a bunch of the audience and the two

girls who shared the podium with them. One time, when Will
came around to her side of the stage, he stopped dead when
he saw her, slapped his hand over his heart, and beat his
chest really fast as if his heart was going to explode. Her
knees went to honey.

She smiled back, then grinned, and then hopped up and
down until Natasha and she were screaming in some kind
of euphoria. He liked her. He really did. Those incredible
kisses meant something. She danced, spinning around, hugging Natasha and the two girls who seemed to be having just
as much fun as she was.

There was no rain dance finale on this show. The boys
closed the show with the same song, "WET", but this time the
stage extended into the audience so all the fans could get to
see the guys a bit closer. Unfortunately, that meant that no
one on the podium could see anything, so Natasha nudged
her down the stairs and backstage.

The boys ran offstage into a room at the side. Natasha
and Anya followed them in. *Wow.*

The guys were bouncing off the walls. Like literally. They
whooped and shouted and high-fived, and double high-fived,
and hugged, and other, slapped one another on the back.
Then Will saw her and shouted, "Anya!"

He picked her up and twirled her around. "You look
totally amazing," he shouted. "Yeah!"

Her feet were a good foot off the ground, but his exuberance was infectious. Again she felt herself caught up in
the pure high in the room. He put her back on the floor
and without warning or hesitation, planted his mouth over
hers. He rushed her backward and held her against the wall.
She could feel every part of him, every part of his body and

every part of his soul as his tongue played with hers, searching, playing, and needing.

"Some fucking Shy Guy," someone said in the room, and as Anya's eyes flew open, everyone paused to look at them. Loud laugher erupted through the small space and, heat infusing her face, she pushed him away from her.

He stepped back, and she smoothed her dress down, looking down to avoid his eyes.

He dipped two fingers under her chin and made her meet his eyes. "Don't be embarrassed. Or if you are embarrassed, get used to it because I intend on kissing you like that every chance I get." He paused, his gaze wandering over her face. "You're phenomenal, and you're mine. Wait. That didn't come out right. I meant I'm yours. If you'll have me."

Her mouth dropped open at such a blatant admission. She stared at him.

"Okay, blink once for no, twice for yes." He grinned.

She blinked twice and he shouted, "Yeah!" again, picking her up and swinging her around. "Wanna split?"

Without waiting for her answer, he grabbed her hand and took off running through the backstage passages. She ran behind him, her hand skimming the walls of the corridor as they ran down them, as if she wanted to reassure herself that this was a real, solid, concrete world and not a crazy, amazing dream that would disappear when she woke up.

Chapter Fourteen

He wasn't sure what his plan was. His brain was too full of the show and the adrenaline to really think it through properly. His brother would be coming to town soon. Anya could never know that she was kissing Matt, not Will.

Which left him with the absolute only answer: he'd have to make Will take over...*everything*. And it made him sick to his stomach.

He'd fucked this one up good and proper. She'd never forgive him for lying to her. Never forgive him for pretending to be Will—and why should she? It's the worst kind of deception, and it was eating him up inside like acid. Slowly but surely corroding his heart.

"Charm her," they'd said. "Make her like you." But they never gave a second thought about what would happen if he liked her back.

He'd come up with a plan tomorrow. Right now, he would explode if he didn't kiss her again. It was like being exposed to her heart, her soul. It tripled his show high. He felt like he could fly when she was in his arms.

He put his hand on the door handle that would take them outside, but before he opened it he spun her around so her back was to the door. He released her hand and stroked the side of her face. She dipped her cheek into his hand, and turned her head so she could kiss his palm.

Electricity spun a live wire web through him like Spider-man. Yeah, he had it bad. *Like bad.*

"Come on, let's get out of here." He opened the door and slipped his arm around her like he'd been born to walk alongside her. She fit perfectly under his shoulder. He could smell the shampoo in her hair without even moving too much. She was like a dream come true.

"Are we going up again?"

"Yup. But I'm grabbing supplies first this time. Give me a sec." He ran to his bus and came out a minute later with a bag and a crisp white duvet that he'd snatched from his bunk. Okay, maybe it was Trevin's bunk, because he'd noticed that he'd had his laundry done that day.

The roof of the arena was much bigger than the last one. They took the walkway all the way around until they could see the sea in the distance. Well, it was just a dark patch, but he assumed it was the sea.

He spread the duvet on the roof and took out soda and his iPhone from his bag. He cued up a playlist he'd pre-pared and hit play. Chill-out music spilled across the roof. "The guys were going into town tonight with crazy Mardi Gras masks on, and I was going to bring you, but I really just wanted to hang with you alone. Hope you don't mind."

"Not at all. I'm not big on crowds," she said, sitting down

and stretching her legs out, arranging her dress carefully over her thighs. *Her thighs*. He looked for a second and then averted his eyes.

"Why not? I mean, you volunteered to cover a tour. Things can get pretty crowded around here. Imagine the other day when we had to hide, multiplied by four."

"Do you find it scary?"

He gazed out into the distance. "More overwhelming than scary. The one thing I'm always scared about is someone else getting hurt in the stampede. It hit us all really bad when that girl fell from the balcony. It could have been so much worse, but to have someone hurt because of the publicity we kind of live and die by. That's hard to stomach."

"Do you want to do this for the rest of your life?" she asked.

"Hell no. I want to go to college and get a good degree in business, because I wouldn't mind learning how to be the manager of a band. Having experienced it, I think I'd be able to steer them better than maybe our manager does." *Shut up. You can't say anything else about LJ.*

"How long have you known that you don't want to be in a band for the rest of your life?"

"Forever? The last few weeks for sure. I don't really know." *Shut up shut up shut up.* "What about you?" He lay on his side, head propped up on his hand. "What do you want to do? Be a reporter?"

She leaned back, supporting herself on her arms. "I thought maybe I could. But I don't know if I have what it takes. College would be a dream, though. That sounds awesome."

So weird he never thought about this before. "Why *aren't* you at college? Where do you live, and who do you live with? I can't believe I don't know these things about you."

She hesitated for a long moment. "Because those are boring things. I'm not at school because I can't afford it, and I don't live with anyone. And Tulsa. There. All the fascinating details." She laughed.

He laughed, too, but it sounded hollow.

"So the tour is going international?" she said.

"Seems to be growing every day. As Natasha said, it started off as a European tour, then they added Japan, now Australia's involved, which will be cool. Who knows what the tour will look like by the time we leave the U.S.? We might never make it back. I call it the 'Making Hay' tour. Don't tell anyone, though."

"You mean making hay while the sun shines? Isn't that what everyone does? Making the most of their popularity, because next year it could be someone else's turn? You're right to get as much money as you can before the next hot thing takes over the charts. It'll definitely fund your degree."

"Right."

He wanted to tell her. To tell her everything about Will, about how he should be pursuing his university dream in a matter of months. But he couldn't risk LJ suing them and putting them all on the streets.

He thought about his mom who, thanks to Will's career, had been able to stop working three jobs for the first time since she'd had the twins. She said she didn't know what to do with herself, but she'd relaxed and looked ten years younger since she was able to stop working. He couldn't take that away from his family, even for the sake of love.

Love? Lust? Intense interest?

He actually had no idea. He just knew that whenever she wasn't in eyesight, he was constantly looking for her. He wanted to kiss her all day, dreamed—uncomfortably—about being bad with her all night.

He closed his eyes for a second to banish that thought. He hadn't brought any cushions. Maybe lying next to each other wasn't the brightest idea.

"Come closer," his hormones said, ignoring his brain.

She shuffled nearer and rested her head on his chest. Perfect. Close, but not pants-tenting close.

"I love…having you right here," he said, wanting to infuse something more intimate into his words without scaring her.

"I love being right here," she murmured back.

He squeezed her closer and said nothing. She soothed him like this. The post-show rush was gone, replaced by something much warmer and calmer. She felt like home. He had no idea why.

. . .

Anya lay with her head on his heart, like she had before, listening to her heartbeat align with his. It felt like the most intimate thing in the world, as if their very existence depended on each other's pulse. Her hand played with his black tie, the last thing he'd worn onstage. "Isn't this uncomfortable?" she whispered, tugging at it gently.

She had a feeling as she said it that she was inviting him to take off some clothes, but she couldn't bring herself to mind or even be scared.

He pushed his fingers in the knot to loosen it and slipped it over his head. "I wouldn't mind losing the shirt, too. It's probably sweaty. Oh God! I'm probably sweaty. I'm so sorry, I didn't even think. Do I smell bad?"

She sat up to allow him to get up, too. "I love how you smell," she said truthfully.

He looked at her for a long second. "I love how you smell, too." He started to unbutton his shirt. "Is it okay if I lose this?"

She bit her lip but nodded. She should say no, right? She should insist on returning to the safety of the Hanging On bus. But she really badly wanted to see him without his shirt.

He stood and pulled the shirt out of his dark blue jeans. His muscles rippled—yup, there was no other word for it—as he threw it onto his bag. He was…a god. A Greek god.

She held out her hand to him, and he took it and pulled her up. Her eyes were glued to his smooth chest. Her hand stretched toward his skin as if it had a mind of its own. She caught it just in time, but he refused to let her retreat and pulled her palm flat against his chest and held his over hers so that his heart throbbed against her hand.

Her knees had no tension, they just felt like liquid. He released her hand and it floated over his pectoral muscles, his abs, and up to his shoulders. She should not be doing this. Should. Not.

Her body disobeyed her brain and in a second, both her hands were on his perfect torso. He closed his eyes and dropped his head. She stroked his tanned arms, his soft skin, actually walking around him, trailing her fingers over his muscles. Her heartbeat seemed to slow in time to her movements, and heat pulsed through her veins.

On his left shoulder was a tattoo. An elaborate compass the size of her hand. But it was partially covered in some kind of waterproof makeup. Maybe he was embarrassed about it? It was beautiful. He was beautiful. He was hers. She kissed between his shoulder blades, and a groan rumbled through his chest. He turned and grabbed her in a bear hug, squeezing the life out of her.

"I don't want to lose you," he said against her hair. "Promise me I won't lose you."

"You won't lose me," she whispered back, not knowing if she was speaking the truth at all. Wouldn't she leave in a couple of weeks? Wouldn't he be leaving for goodness knew how long on his world tour? And that was only assuming she wasn't fired on the spot if Cynthia found out the truth about her.

It didn't seem the right time or place to question his words. To dig for a deeper, more permanent meaning. And even if she'd wanted to, he chose that moment to kiss her, and all sensible thoughts left her mind.

As his lips pressed her mouth open, she stroked his back, loving the feel of his skin under her hands. His muscles flexed as if they were vying for her to touch them. She wanted to touch every part of him.

A new playlist came from his phone, this time more upbeat. He stopped kissing her and pulled her close to him, dancing in time to the faster music. He pushed her away and held her hands, spinning her around and dipping her until he was laughing and she was shrieking every time he dipped her and pressed a kiss to her neck.

Eventually they stopped dancing, sweaty and out of breath in the humid night air. They collapsed to the duvet and lay down together. His breath came in pants, as did hers. She lay her head back on his chest. They'd talk when they'd got their breath back.

In just a minute.

Chapter Fifteen

Matt was carrying her downstairs in his arms when she woke.

"Put me down," she whispered. "What happened?"

He continued until they reached a landing, and then he put her down. She rubbed her eyes with her fists, totally adorably, like a kid. When she pulled her hands away, she looked like a panda with black eye makeup down to her cheek. He grinned. "Nothing happened. You were dead to the world and it started to rain. So I figured I'd just carry you back to your bus. But we might get less wet now that you're awake."

He led her to the door outside, which he opened. It was raining torrentially. Like an Armageddon movie rainstorm. He could barely see outside.

He braced the door open with his foot and turned to her. "Now tell me truthfully. If you get wet, you're not going to melt or anything, are you?"

She punched him in the chest. "Are you insinuating that

I'm the Wicked Witch of the West?"

"West. East. Can't a guy just double-check before the worst happens?"

"Oh you…you…"

He ran out into the rain, leaving her holding the door. He'd left everything on the roof except his phone, which he'd stuffed into his pocket. Instantly, he was soaked. He swore it was the same pressure as a good shower.

He held his hand out to her, and she ran to him, holding herself stiff for a moment as the rain hit her. Then she looked up at him. Her hair flat and her makeup seriously running in rivulets down her cheek. She still looked freaking amazing. He kissed her gently on her forehead, lingering like he was trying to absorb her into him.

Voices came from near the barrier. They both looked toward the noise. Someone was singing. No, a bunch of people were singing. They moved closer, and he tried to see what was going on through the rain.

"Oh my God," Anya said. "Go join."

Laughter erupted. The other guys, with their stupid masks now on top of their heads, were singing and dancing to "WET" in front of the group of girls who'd been standing vigil at the gate with their posters. The crowd started to sing, too. He thought he'd seen it all.

He kissed Anya's hand, then ran over. Miles did a double take and high-fived him when he took his place at the end of the line.

They danced and sang for the crowd of girls, who for once were singing and not screaming. They kicked water at them, at the people who had accompanied the others downtown, and at one another. They laughed and sang. The guys working security at the gate were clapping to keep time. He sang his heart out. Sang for Anya and the girls who had been waiting all day to catch a glimpse of Seconds to Juliet.

The song ended and Ryder shouted, "And they told us you couldn't get WET in New Orleans!" The crowd cheered as the five guys passed down the line, shaking hands, posing for photos and high-fiving the people farther back in the crowd.

"That was awesome!" Anya said when he'd run back to her.

"Right? I've never seen fans so happy." He grinned and spun her around. "Let's get you out of those clothes."

Her beautiful, if totally panda-like, eyes widened.

"Not what I meant. Unless…" He winked at her.

She rolled her eyes.

The other guys ran to The One. Miles lost his mask and had to double back to grab it from the ground before sprinting to get out of the rain.

Matt walked her to the bottom of the steps of her bus. "I'll leave you here, sweetheart. I had an awesome night. I want to tell you that I love…spending time with you." He couldn't resist a grin.

She swallowed and said, "I love…spending time with you, too." She punctuated it by sticking out her tongue at him.

"Show me that again." His heart raced. Would she?

She did. She poked her tongue out, and he swooped down to pull it into his mouth. A few seconds later they broke apart, both breathing heavier. "Sweet dreams, Anya." He winked again and jumped back down the stairs. He stood there watching her, hands in her pockets, until she shut the door.

He was seriously fucked.

. . .

Anya leaned against the door after she closed it. She shook herself all over and couldn't help but squeak. She shook her fists and danced through the trailer. Best. Day. Ever. She spun around and around, holding her arms out wide. Perfect day. Perfect boy. Perfect day.

She took off her sodden dress and hung it over the back of a chair in the galley kitchen, snuggling into her tank and shorts. Life, for once, was great. The greatest. How had her world so completely turned around so fast? She'd always believed that she'd only ever have bad luck and had blamed her mom for a lot of that.

Her tablet lay on the booth table, and she realized that she must have left it with Natasha. She swiped the screen and paged through photos from the show. Her heart jumped when she saw the photo of Will holding his hand over his heart when he'd seen her in her dress. Natasha must have taken it. It was perfect. He was beautiful. And he looked at her as if *she* was beautiful, too.

She sighed with happiness and opened her WowSounds blog, wondering which photos to post tomorrow. The third comment caught her eye.

Good news! We've found him and are looking after him you-know-where. FH.

Father Howard! And the name the post was actually attributed to was *JudetheWanderer*.

There was no way this day could get any better. No effing way. She collapsed over the tablet, her whole body heaving with relief. Everything, absolutely everything was good in her world right now. Better than good. Natasha, her meeting with Cyn, Will, Jude. The planets had aligned for once in her favor, and it felt huge.

She grabbed her notebook and scribbled some Will information.

Memory issues (Nathan and The Tudors*) – face-plant related?*

Knows precisely zero about the world tour.

Bone structure changed since said face-plant.

She shimmied into bed, wriggled her toes, her legs, and then her whole body against the smooth white sheets and grinned in the dark.

Life was good.

Except…

Hold the phone.

Something was…off. But what was it?

Didn't it make sense that some things *wouldn't* make sense? He was a rock star. He was allowed his quirks.

But still, some vital clue tickled the back of her mind—

She jumped up and turned on the light.

The night they'd spent at the back of her bus, Will had rubbed his right knee. But in the photos online, she'd seen a bandage around his left knee. There had to be an explanation, right? Maybe they'd transposed the photo?

She grabbed her notebook from under her pillow and went out to the kitchen and booted up the tablet. She opened her book to the Will fact page and read them all in one go. She rubbed her eyes. Read them again. There was only one thing missing.

She went back to the high school website where she'd

found Alice Singleton earlier. She squinted at other candid photos, one after the other, seeing who was tagged in them.

Then there were two boys dressed up like Luke Skywalker and Princess Leia for Halloween. She knew that Luke Skywalker was Will as soon as she saw it. It was tagged with Matt Fray and Will Fray. Will had a brother. She should probably have known that. She giggled again at Princess Leia.

She scrolled through some older photos, wondering if there'd be another one of Will. Way, way back in the archive she found a picture of the brothers again. She started at how similar they looked without makeup. She took a sharp intake of breath as she read the tag: Evil Twin and Eviler Twin.

They were twins.

Their hair was a bit different, one was grinning, and one looked nervous. One wore a T-shirt and one looked uncomfortable in a button-down. But when you squeezed your fingers into a tight circle and placed them over the photos so only their faces showed...yes. Nearly identical. She couldn't tell them apart.

Couldn't tell them apart.

She reread her list of Will facts and started scribbling, heart racing. Mounting anger made her handwriting shake.

Had he been lying to her the whole time?

About everything?

He wasn't who he said he was. Could she be right? And if so, who knew? Who else knew that Matt was pretending to be Will? She fought her impulse to go bang on the door of The One, but Will/Matt had some serious explaining to do in the morning. That is, if she could bear to speak to him again.

She sat back in her chair and gazed out of the window

into the darkness. A chilled finger poked her spine.

Had he really been lying about everything? Everything?

"I told you. Didn't I tell you?"

The voice screeched into her sleep and yanked her awake. She'd lain awake all night, unable to shake the truth she'd realized about Will. She must have finally fallen asleep out of pure exhaustion.

She peered out of the curtains to find LJ and...who was that? The girl from Cherry? In the trailer?

Anya half climbed and half fell out of the bunk, bashing her head at the same time. She straightened, rubbing her forehead.

LJ looked her up and down. "Mrs. Anderson?" His expression made it obvious he knew she wasn't a Mrs. anything. He sighed. "Is this your dress?" He held up the still sopping wet, gold dress from the kitchen chair between two fingers.

"No sir. Nat...er, I...it was borrowed from the costume department last night. I was told that it was a rejected costume." The words sounded stupid even to her.

"I. Told. You," Paige said, arms crossed in front of her and foot tapping on the floor.

LJ rolled his eyes. "I'm afraid, Mrs. Anderson, that Ms. Parker here reported it as stolen last night. Natasha was fired and escorted from the premises. And I will be in touch with your editor to make sure that WowSounds pays for the cost of the dress."

The whole world fell in. "How much does the dress cost?" she stammered.

"About $1500," Paige said triumphantly. "It's a Valentino."

It might as well have been three million.

"That'll teach you to hang out with people who are rude to me," Paige said. "I'm the talent around here, not the stupid makeup girl."

"All right, enough. We'll let you get dressed." LJ spun around and ushered Paige from the trailer, although she couldn't resist turning around and sending Anya a truly smug smile.

The door slammed, and Anya rubbed her eyes. She pulled back Natasha's bunk curtain to find it empty. She looked at the clock on the microwave in the kitchen and was horrified to find it read nearly eleven a.m.

She collapsed on the edge of a chair and put her head in her hands. She'd gotten Natasha fired? Natasha was gone?

Her heart sank. She felt awful. Bone crushingly, stomach achingly bad. And then she realized that there was no one to help her get through her meeting with Cyn, or to take her place at it. And if LJ did call her, she'd be out of a job anyway, with her per diems eaten up by the cost of the dress.

But it didn't matter. She'd been expelled from the tour, so what did it matter if Cyn also fired her?

In the space of twelve hours, she was back where she was before she got here. A familiar nausea rose in her stomach like an old friend. She never puked—she rarely had had enough food to puke anything anyway—the feeling just stayed with her constantly. But these past days it had all but disappeared.

And now the sensation was back with a vengeance, and she felt the weight of the impossibility of her situation even more. This was her fault. She'd gotten caught up in the excitement of everything. Of having a boy like her.

Crap.

Matt. Will. Instantly, everything she'd discovered in the middle of the night flooded back.

How would LJ like it if she ran and told him that Will and Matt were lying to him? How would Paige feel if she suddenly had no band to be the supporting act for?

He'd lied to her. He'd lied about everything. His past, Alice Singleton… She had no idea if any of what he'd told her was true. Heat flooded through her. How stupid did he think she was? Kissing him, falling for a lie. Falling for *him*. He must have been laughing at her every night.

She snatched on some clothes and ran out of the trailer. The SUVs that normally sat next to The One had disappeared. They were all probably out at an interview or something. She bolted to the bus anyway and thumped on the door. No one answered. She tried again.

Nothing.

She had to leave. She couldn't wait for him to get back. He might be gone all day. She had to make the meeting with Cyn—it was the right thing to do, even if she threw herself on her mercy.

In the Hanging On bus, she packed her things as fast as possible, pausing only to email herself the photo of Will—Matt—looking up at her from the stage. If she lost everything, at least she'd have that as proof to herself that she'd been here. Leaving everything that wasn't strictly hers, she heaved her bags onto her back, paused to look around, and left.

Every step she took reinforced her belief that she'd been

stupid. She was too embarrassed to leave a note for Will. Or Matt. Or whatever the hell she should call him.

How do you write a, "Sorry, I was busted for stealing that dress you liked me in last night, and how dare you lie to me and treat me like I was nothing" note? And she had no idea how to get in contact with Natasha to apologize.

She knew this job was too good to be true. She knew Will was too good to be true. She didn't deserve Natasha's friendship. She didn't deserve a break. She didn't deserve anything. Just like her mom had always said.

The threat of tears bubbled in her throat when she thought about Will or Matt, or whoever had called her his girlfriend. And then she let anger push through.

Anger was better than tears.

Chapter Sixteen

Matt was getting antsy. They were at an interview at a local radio station and it was going well, but all he could think about was getting back to Anya.

The questions were getting banal. Questions that'd been asked and answered a million times. Maybe more. Why did Ryder write "Kiss This"? How did Miles manage to persuade the band to sing that song to Aimee?

Jeez, man. Let me Google that for you.

"And Will," the DJ asked, dragging him out of his thoughts. "Some people who enjoyed the band's impromptu number last night in the rain, said that you had been kissing a girl right before joining in. Who was that? A fan? Are you off the market now?"

Every face turned to him. Nathan looked petrified. If Matt said he was taken, that'd leave Nathan holding the hopes and dreams of every single girl in his lone, unattached hands. Behind the glass, LJ drew a finger across his throat.

Oh, how he'd love to piss him off just to see his face. But he had to think about the real Will. He forced a laugh.

"Sometimes you just want to kiss a pretty girl, you know?"

The DJ laughed. "Absolutely nothing wrong with that, Will. Who could blame you?"

Nathan looked so relieved that Matt almost laughed at him. Poor Nathan. Even LJ looked satisfied.

"So you and Nathan are the only two single members of the band now. Are you worried that being attached may reduce your fan base significantly?" the DJ asked.

They had a stock answer to that, and luckily Matt never had to deliver it. Trevin took that one. "You know, we've found our fans stick with us through thick and thin, and frankly—we all agree—no one gets between us and our fans. We'd be nothing without them."

The band's job here was to interject "Yes," "Absolutely," and "We love our fans," in a chorus of agreement. They all did it perfectly, so it sounded spontaneous. LJ had them well trained. Like dogs on leashes, Matt thought.

He took an offered coffee as the station played one of their new tracks, again written by Ryder. They were all turning into songwriters, and it made the band sound way more authentic. Maybe they weren't destined to be trivia questions ten years from now. Maybe they would segue their fame into a real band that he knew the others really wanted.

Matt just couldn't wait to let his hair grow again and take up the place he'd been offered at FSU. And somehow get Anya into his life without letting on that… Yeah, he still hadn't sorted that one out.

Thirty minutes later, they were signing photos, notebooks, and phone covers outside the radio station, posing for photos, and kissing cheeks. After twenty minutes or so, their security team came over to escort them back into their transportation. They always worked it that way so it appeared that the band didn't have a choice but to leave.

The SUVs took them the short distance back to the stadium and dumped them all at the door to The One.

Matt took off toward Hanging On, but as he got closer he saw a team of cleaners traipsing up and down the stairs with trash bags, vacuums, and bucket and mops. Huh. Well, Anya wouldn't be in there if they were deep-cleaning it. Maybe she was in the makeup trailer with Natasha. He ducked in the door.

Someone was there. Shit. He recognized the face. Will had shown him photos of everyone on tour before he'd taken his place. She was…oh crap…the sick makeup artist who Natasha was filling in for. What was her name? Dammit. It wouldn't come to him; he'd have to wing it. "Are you better?"

She turned and gave a wan smile. "Nope. Not really." She pressed her hand to her stomach and sneezed, almost doubling over and groaning in pain.

Matt ran to help her to a seat. "Jesus. What happened to you?"

"It's Murphy's Law, babe. I got a cold just after I had the operation. Every time I cough or sneeze, or move fast, it feels like my stiches are being yanked out. It's hell."

"So what are you doing here? I thought they'd given you like a couple of months off." He sat down next to her and handed her a bottle of water.

"They had. Paige Parker made some kind of scene and insisted that LJ fire Natasha and some reporter girl. They left last night, I think, because at midnight I got a call to come back"—her voice changed to a spot-on impersonation of LJ—"Deb...we need you back before tonight! Deb... you'll get a raise!" She rolled her eyes. "A raise? From LJ? I had to come back and see what *that* was like."

Deb. Right.

And then he realized what she'd said. His jaw dropped. "Both of them left last night?" he asked.

"I don't know, babe, you now know as much as I do. I guess so? They were the only ones staying in Hanging On and they're cleaning the whole place, I think. I got my old bunk back in Rock You."

Matt stood, not knowing what to do with himself. He paced a bit. And then stopped.

"What's wrong?" Deb asked. "You're making me dizzy."

"Nothing. Sorry, I've got to go. Feel better." Matt went for the door. "Shit. By the way. Move into Hanging On. Since you left, the shocks on the Rock You bus got worse. It'll be hell if you're in pain."

"Thanks for the advice," she shouted behind him as he left.

He barged into Hanging On. He had to see if she'd left him a note or anything. He asked the cleaners and they said the only thing that had been left was the tablet on the kitchen table.

He looked around desperately, in case there was a note or anything. He went to her bunk and swiped the curtain open. A waft of her vanilla shampoo enveloped him and he nearly effing sobbed with frustration. He thumped the pillow and banged his hand on something hard. She'd left her notebook. He pulled it out. Maybe there was an address in it.

The book flopped open to a page in the middle where

the pen was. WILL FACTS was written on the top line and written over and over like a doodle. He smiled, until he read his facts.

Off the record girlfriends?

Psycho Fans. This is true. Reference comments on blog!!!

"They banded together…" Distant from the others? Because he isn't Will?

Fried Bread? Blerg.

Vegetarian? Maybe Will's a veggie and Matt isn't. Slip up?

Needle phobia—passes out! And yet has a partially hidden tattoo on shoulder. Matt?

Alice Singleton first girlfriend. She'd be able to confirm surely?

Will and Nathan the only singles left on the tour.

Kissed Natasha at the beginning of the tour. And yet doesn't seem to remember it?

Twisted his right knee. Photo of left knee in bandages on TMZ.

Says he hasn't kissed anyone on the tour. (lie) Unless Will did, and Matt didn't. Until me?

Definitely kisses on the first date. (see Natasha)

Has had sex before. Wonder who with?

Memory issues. (Nathan and the Tudors) – face-plant related? Nope. Obvs Will told Nathan about *The Tudors.* Matt had no idea.

Knows precisely zero about the world tour.

Bone structure changed since said face-plant. Occam's razor. It's not Will, it's Matt.

He slammed the notebook shut and looked around as if someone might have been watching him. When had she put these clues together? When had she first suspected? Had she made him fall in love with her just for a scoop? The exclusive breaking news? Nausea rushed through him and he sat down. Fuck.

Images of his brother and mother on the streets. A fate he couldn't even imagine before now had become vivid in his mind. LJ would own them all. Totally and forever. He'd screwed up and screwed them all. He looked at his watch and wondered how long he'd have before she filed her story. It could already be up.

He checked his phone while pacing the bus. There was nothing on WowSounds. Maybe she'd gone for a larger audience. A better payday. He Google searched "news + Will Fray". Nothing new came up.

He rushed back to the band's bus and ran up the stairs, banging the door open.

Immediately, a magazine came flying through the air. He dodged it.

"How many times have you been told, do *not* bang the door," Ryder said, his calm voice belying his words.

Matt ignored him. "Was there a note left for me anywhere?"

The guys frowned and looked around. "Not that I can see," Trevin said. "What's up?"

Matt just flopped down on the sofa and said nothing. His mind was running at a million miles an hour. He had no way of finding her. He didn't know where she lived, not even the city. The only thing he knew about her was that she worked at WowSounds. His stomach started to rebel in the same way it had when he'd answered the knock on the door at home at three o'clock in the morning and found Will high and desperate.

"Dude. Put your head between your legs, you look like you're about to pass out." Trevin jumped up and shoved Matt's head down.

After a second, he began to feel better and picked up his head. All four members were in the kitchen watching him. "What happened, mate?" Miles asked. "Are you sick?"

He couldn't tell them. He couldn't spill about Will. He just…wanted to lie down in his bunk and disappear.

Would Anya really leave without a word?

Of course she would. She'd gotten what she'd come for.

Dammit. It had felt real. Really real.

A hollowness burrowed into his heart. Never again would he trust his own feelings. He looked at his fists clenched on his lap.

He had to get his shit together.

"Paige Parker got Natasha fired last night, and Anya's disappeared, too. They're gone, and I've got no way of contacting either of them. Especially Anya."

"Oh sweet Jesus," Ryder said. "Hey, Trevin. That's twenty bucks. I told you he was in love with that reporter girl. 'Oh no,' you said. 'He wouldn't do that.' Cough up."

Trevin handed him a twenty dollar bill, shaking his head at Matt.

"You bet on me?" Matt asked weakly.

"Oh please. It was barely a bet. I mean, it was totally inevitable." Ryder grinned as he stuffed the bill into his back pocket.

"So what are you going to do?" Nathan asked. "Paige is horrible. She was always nasty to me. Natasha was always lovely. We should do something."

"Paige was nasty to you?" Trevin said. "Why didn't you

tell me? I'd have made her back off in a heartbeat."

Nathan shrugged, eyes on a computer in the middle of the table.

It was only in the silence that Matt heard a song coming from the PC. "Who's that?"

Miles spun the screen around. "We were watching this girl on YouTube. She's done this awesome cover of The One. We all just tweeted it."

Matt looked at the screen. She was a pretty young girl. All fresh-faced and ponytailed, sitting on her bed with a guitar. She was good. Really good. "Nice," he agreed weakly before flopping back onto the sofa.

"So let's summarize," Ryder began. "You're in love with the reporter tasked to dig up dirt on you. Somehow you managed to fall in love with her without knowing how to get in contact with her—"

"Seriously? Did you not exchange phone numbers, emails, and Instagram handles? Nothing?" Miles asked.

Matt shook his head as Ryder continued. "LJ would have a fit if you publicly dated her anyway, as would Nathan, and speaking of whom, LJ and the bitch from bitchville just fired Natasha, who I think we can all agree was an asset to the crew, and the love of your life has disappeared. Did I forget anything?"

"D'you think she dug up some scandal and ran off to report it?" Nathan asked, looking around. "Who's been bad, then? Which of you was it?"

Matt nearly choked.

Chapter Seventeen

Anya had gotten to the café early and had spent one of her last dollars on a cup of tea. She slunk down in her chair as she recognized the voices on the radio. Seconds to Juliet was doing an interview. Will wasn't saying anything at all. Until he did. A tear leaked down her face when she heard him say that sometimes he just wanted to kiss a pretty girl.

Well, at least he said she was pretty. But that was all on Natasha. It was she who'd made Anya look so special last night. Damn him for all his lies and for making her feel stupid. And hurt.

A lady walked into the nearly empty café and looked around, her gaze skimming over Anya and moving on. She recognized her editor from her photo on the website. So she stood up and waved. "Mrs. Wilson? Cyn?"

A shocked look came over her face as she nodded and threaded her way through the empty tables toward her. She stopped at the table and stared at her for a good long moment. Her mouth twitched. "Anya Anderson?"

"I'm afraid so."

She pulled out the chair and sat down, her gaze still on Anya. "Wow," she said. "Not *exactly* what I was expecting."

"I know. I'm sorry. I think I kind of messed up." So much was bound up inside Anya that she decided to get it all out on the table so she could just apologize and move on.

"I did get a call from S2J's manager telling me that I owed him fifteen hundred dollars for a dress. So maybe, yes, you did mess up. Tell me that you got a story. Some kind of a tell-all story that will make all this worthwhile."

Anya swallowed. "I did find out something…"

Cynthia raised her eyebrows. "Well? What was it?"

What did she say to that? Just blurt out the truth? Besides…

"I'm not sure if it's the right story for WowSounds."

Her editor sighed. "In that case, I'm sorry, Mrs. Anderson—"

"It's just Anya. No husband, no kids." She pulled a contrite face.

Mrs. Wilson shook her head. "I'm sorry, but if you don't have a story by now, I've got no more use for you."

"If you give me more time, maybe I can—"

"No. Their manager asked me to pull you. And if you can't stay with the tour, I can't pay you anymore. Your click rate has allowed us to raise our advertising prices for your blog, so I won't pass on the charge of the dress, and I have a check for you for your per diems." She took out an envelope. "Four hundred dollars. Good-bye, Anya. Sorry it didn't work out." She held out her hand. "The tablet?"

Anya winced. "I'm sorry, I left it in the bus I was staying on."

Mrs. Wilson picked up the envelope with the check inside it and said, "You'll get this back when you return my tablet. I'm staying at the Meridian Hotel until tomorrow morning. Leave the tablet at the front desk before tonight, and they'll give you this. Okay?"

Anya nodded, but inside she was desperate for a solution. If it had just been her future on the line, maybe she could have walked away. But this wasn't just about her future. It was about Jude's, too. She couldn't let him down now.

Cynthia stood and picked up her handbag—

"Mrs. Wilson, wait…"

Cynthia stopped and raised her eyebrows. "Having second thoughts?"

"What if I could give you the story of a lifetime?" Her stomach churned as she said the words.

Her boss—or maybe ex-boss—crossed her arms. "Go on."

"It's big. Maybe enough to break up the band." Bile rose in her chest. What was she doing?

After a long moment, Cynthia shrugged. "Fine. It's on you. Bring me the tablet or bring me the story." With that, she turned and walked away.

The story or the tablet.

The truth or nothing at all.

She patted her backpack for her notebook to reread the clues that would convince everyone she wasn't making this all up. It wasn't there? How could she have forgotten it?

Either way, now she would have to trek all the way back to the stadium and all the way back again. What would she do if she ran into Will, or Matt, or whoever he was? She'd have to be quick. In and out before anyone saw her.

She gathered her things and picked up a tourist map from a black wire stand at the door of the café so that she would be able to find her way to the hotel.

Maybe she could time it so that he'd be in makeup or costume when she arrived. She didn't want to see him. She'd be too embarrassed. She'd been thrown off the tour for stealing a dress, and he'd spent the last week lying to her. Anyway, he'd probably forgotten all about her by now. What had he said? Just a pretty girl.

She wanted to believe he had feelings for her, that at least *that* part had been true, but she knew better than anyone how thick a web of lies could be. Where did his deception begin and end? Even if he insisted his feelings for her were real, how would she know what to believe when he said one thing in private, another in public?

As she walked slowly under the weight of her backpack, she actually wished that she'd had sex with him. Just that one time. Because she'd never felt like she wanted to before, and she wasn't sure now she would ever feel that way again. Just to feel loved for that moment, maybe that would have seen her through…everything to come.

Maybe that would have made this decision so much easier.

But she hadn't slept with him. And unless she retrieved her notebook and wrote this story, she'd have nothing to show for the whole horrible mess.

The streets got less and less crowded the farther she got from downtown, and the second she rounded a corner into a totally deserted road, she slumped against a wall. Dry sobs racked her body. She bent over, telling herself that it wasn't crippling despair but the weight of her pack that felt unbearable.

Enough. Enough. You've been through worse. You've escaped worse. You can survive.

She straightened and wiped her nose on her T-shirt sleeve, since that was the only thing she could reach. Everything inside her wanted to turn around and go nowhere near the stadium, but what would help her and Jude more? A few hundred dollars would only get them so far. A job—a *real* job—would help them for a lot longer.

She pushed her shoulders back, readjusted her pack, and started walking again. With every step, she raised her chin.

As she drew close, she dug around for her backstage pass to show the guy at the security gate. Luckily, she'd kept it as a memento. She'd actually fought herself about it as she'd hastily packed. She wanted to remember this past week, but on the other hand, everything had been screwed up so badly, she also kind of wanted to walk away. To pretend it hadn't happened at all.

Okay, chin up, chin up.

She approached the gate and held out the pass that she'd slipped around her neck. The guy who had first shown her in a lifetime ago nodded at her and went back to his monitors. She pressed through the barrier and paused. Everything looked exactly the same, but everything felt totally different. She didn't belong here anymore.

No one was outside the trailers, not that it was really surprising. It was steaming hot. There was a yellow warning sign outside the Hanging On bus that indicated someone had cleaned the floors in there. She hoped the tablet and notebook were still there. She carefully maneuvered up the steps with her backpack, which almost stopped her getting through the door. That would add insult to injury right there. For a second, she imagined herself stuck in the door, unable to free herself, arms waving like a cockroach on its back.

She managed to get in and grab the tablet, which was exactly where she'd left it. Thank God. After stowing it in a side pocket, she checked her bunk for her notebook. Gone. Dammit. She didn't have time to chase down whoever cleaned the bus. She peered out the window to make sure she could make a clean break to the security gate again. It was still deserted.

She took one last look around the trailer that had felt like her home, even though she'd only been in it for a few days, opened the door, and broke for the border.

She'd made it halfway to freedom when a door slammed and raised voices floated on the breeze toward her. She made the mistake of looking around. It was Paige, clutching the gold dress, and Will or Matt…or maybe she should just start thinking of his as 'Fray'. Her heart stopped, and everything seemed to slow down.

The dress floated gently in the air as Paige brandished it, the sparkles catching the fading sunlight. She remembered how she'd felt when she'd worn it. But now she knew that Fray was getting the scoop about her stealing it. Could she get away?

No. His eyes met hers and, like a magnet, she felt drawn to him. Couldn't move away. Even as he grabbed the dress, pointed at Paige to go, and strode across the parking lot, she couldn't move. Even though she knew it was over, her feet were welded to the concrete. Her body, mind, and heart were obviously longing for the torment of this end, this breakup, otherwise they'd let her run.

He stood in front of her, and she swayed toward him. He said nothing for a second, but his eyes looked as stormy as the clouds gathering over the stadium.

"Did you steal this?" he asked, not even holding up the dress for her to see.

"I…" Her voice broke, and no sound emerged. She cleared her throat. "I didn't mean to." She didn't want to mention Natasha. Didn't want to get her into any more trouble.

"When you left, you forgot this." His words were as hard as steel. He took something out of his back pocket. Her notebook. "You were going to screw me and the band with some wild story about my twin? Are you just really working for a sleazy tabloid? Was I some game?" He gestured between them, but the twist in his mouth said that it hurt for him to think about them together. "Was *this* some game?"

"No. *No*. I—"

"Don't. You had all these theories, but you never once asked me about them. Was that deliberate? So I couldn't deny your story? So you could just publish it without any comment?"

She started to shake. This was so out of control, she didn't know how to fix it. How to explain. Because the truth was that yes, she had arrived on the tour with every hope of getting the scoop on him. With every intention of selling her story to the highest bidder so that she could get herself and Jude somewhere safe. And until this moment, she'd still wondered if she could go through with the plan. She couldn't deny it. Not without lying.

But wait a minute. Her anger at him bubbled to the surface again. "Why would I have asked you for a comment when all you'd do was lie? That's all you've ever told me, isn't it? A bunch of lies. Lies on top of lies. What is it that people say? 'I can tell you're lying because your lips are moving.' Why would you tell me the truth about anything? You even lied about your *name*."

She was so going to write this story.

She hauled her backpack higher almost in defiance. But his face was all wrong. He looked hurt, sad, and angry, all at the same time.

She was so not going to write this story. Just like she knew that even thinking about betraying him had sealed her fate from the beginning.

She'd ruined everything. Everything. And now he hated her, thought she was a thief and worse. She could see it clearly in his eyes.

"What do you care? You were probably going to kiss and tell anyway, weren't you? I can't believe I…" He shook his head.

"What? You can't believe you what?" Her heart beat faster with the possibility that—

"Nothing. Just go." He looked at the ground. "And please, don't come back."

She'd been wrong last night. She hadn't imagined a tenth of what this felt like. Not even a little.

Anya slowly turned from him, taking one last look at the boy she loved. He was still holding the dress that had gotten both her and Natasha fired.

Nothing in her seventeen years had prepared her for this. Every part of her felt broken, and there was no one who could help her put the pieces back together.

She was alone. Again.

Anya wanted to cry, but instead of sadness, a cold emptiness filled her. She didn't even have the energy to wipe her eyes or pretend everything was okay. It was all she could do to keep walking and not curl up in an alley and pretend she was invisible.

She stopped long enough to turn on the tablet and erase her notes. She wouldn't expose Will's secrets, and as far as she was concerned, no one else ever would, either.

She needed to get her check and leave. Pretend this hadn't happened. Move on, forget. Except she had the awful fear that she'd never forget the memory of him telling her to leave and never come back.

She reached the hotel. The guy behind the desk told her that no one had left anything for her, but that Mrs. Wilson hadn't come back since she'd left that morning.

Anya collapsed into a lobby armchair after attempting to hide her backpack behind its neighboring sofa. She didn't want people to look at her, and she was painfully aware that no one checking in or out of the hotel had a large unwieldy backpack for luggage. They were all sleek, wheeled, and expensive-looking.

For ten minutes, she watched the door, hoping that Mrs. Wilcox would arrive. Then Anya could head to the bus station. She checked the map in vain for the location of a bank en route to her bus, so she could cash the check.

When Mrs. Wilcox eventually came, Anya handed over the tablet without a word. Which said it all, didn't it? No story. It was over.

Mrs. Wilcox didn't say much. Just gave her the check and

turned around, shaking her head. She was probably making a mental note to meet all her freelance reporters in the future.

As soon as she stepped out of the hotel, thunder rolled, and rain poured. Of course it would be raining. Because there was no way she could catch a break. She had $375 in her pocket, and she had spent the past fifteen minutes cursing out the hotel receptionist who had charged her $25 for cashing the check. And now she was wet.

Actually, "wet" didn't cover the magnitude of water that had been soaked up by her clothes, backpack, hair, and skin. She felt as if she were carrying an extra ten pounds in rainwater alone. And the straps were killing her shoulders. They would be blistered later.

It doesn't matter. Nothing matters. I'm on my way home.

Twenty minutes later, it was with some relief that she realized the ticket office at the bus station was actually in a building. Often they were just booths outside. She went inside and then sighed. There was a ticket seller and three chairs in a waiting room, all of them taken.

"One to Tulsa, Oklahoma please," she said.

He didn't look up at her, just took her money and passed her a ticket. "Change in Dallas. Bus leaves in six minutes."

At last, some luck. She'd been worried she'd have to wait half a day, or worse, for the bus to leave. She elected to go outside so she could find the right bus stop. She really didn't want to miss it. She was getting the hell out of Dodge.

Brakes squeaked as the bus pulled up. A stream of people got off, then paused to get their luggage. Anya pulled her bags from her shoulders and stood by the baggage hold.

"Slow your roll, sweetheart," the driver said. "I'm switching out. The new driver will take your bags and ticket." He shut the door with a lever on the outside of the bus and left her standing in the rain. Yup. That was how she was rolling: slow…and wet.

But at least no one could tell the difference between the rain and her tears.

Chapter Eighteen

Matt looked at his watch. It had been exactly five hours since their argument—not that he was counting—and still there was no tell-all story. Not even a hint of "Seconds to Juliet breaking news coming soon!" notifications.

Had he misjudged her?

Because even if she'd believed his lame denial of being Will's twin, she still had a bunch of ammunition…him joking about Miles being gay; their relationship…because yes, it had been a relationship; the stupid jokes about the industry insiders and their terrible dancing. Nothing hideous, but still, enough to embarrass the band. And him. Enough to make her story a way in to a bigger publication.

He'd been so stupid to push her away. He should have given her time to talk. Maybe he should have confided in her. Taken that leap of faith.

It was probably too late now. She'd go back to her life and forget about him.

Fuck. He hated that thought. But what else was he supposed to do? Wasn't his sacrifice necessary to protect the
band? Just because she hadn't posted the story didn't mean
she wouldn't.

They were all sitting on the bus, waiting to head out to
that night's performance. They had about an hour or so until
showtime.

"No word?" Nathan asked for the hundredth time. He
was such a cool guy. He seemed really concerned about Anya
and him, even though if "Will" hooked up with someone, it
would leave him to carry the single S2Jer banner alone.

"Nothing. But also no story. At least not yet, anyway."

"Seriously, mate, did you do something that she might
have run off to report on?" Miles asked.

This wasn't the first time he'd been asked, and usually
they all butted in with things they suspected he might have
done. But none of them said anything. He looked up and
saw everyone except Trevin staring over Matt's shoulder.

"Yeah, he might have done. But anyway, I think it's time
to start using our powers for good, don't you think?" said a
voice Matt knew only too well.

"What the actual fuck?" Ryder asked, echoing what all
the others were most likely thinking.

Matt stood up, turned around, and looked his twin brother up and down. He couldn't suppress a grin. It was good to
see him. And in such good shape. "Dude." He opened his
arms and Will strode up and hugged him.

"Thanks. I…just thanks, bro," he said quietly.

"No need. It's good to see your filthy, ugly face again,"
Matt said, trying to veer away from any emotional reunion
conversations in front of the others. The others. He looked

around at the guys, of whom only Trevin looked amused.

"What's this? Some kind of freak-show 'Parent Trap'?" Ryder seemed to be the only one who hadn't been struck dumb by double vision.

Will held his hands up in a conciliatory gesture. "I'm sorry. I'm really sorry, but I was in such trouble with those pain pills LJ gave me, and then when my mom insisted I go to rehab, he threatened to sue her for loss of earnings and breach of contract. This was literally our only option."

"That's amazing," Miles said. "I wondered why you'd forget lyrics that you wrote. You are so freaking identical." He shook his head in wonder and peered harder. "Wait. No you're not. Now that you're both together I can see you're different. I just never noticed it before. But you're okay now, Will?"

"Yeah. I really am. Knee's still a bit sore, but I just have to put up with that now," his brother said.

"Well, who are you then?" Nathan asked, brow still furrowed. "I feel like I should know Will's brother's name, but I don't."

"I'm Matt," he said, relieved that it was all out in the open, but still worried that someone could roll on them. He looked at Trevin, who nodded.

"Guys, are we all agreed to support Will now?" Trevin said. "No grassing him up, no getting his family sued?"

"Bloody hell, of course," Miles said. "They might be twins, but we're all brothers. Am I right?" He looked around at the others and held out his fist, as they did every night before they went onstage.

Everyone leaned in to knock fists. Matt hesitated after Will leaned in, wondering if he was still included, but they all waited from him to join before whispering "Whaaaa" and pulling their hands back.

"So what seems to be the trouble?" Will asked, sitting next to Matt.

"Nice wife-beater, bro." Matt raised his eyebrows and shook his head, as if he couldn't believe his twin would wear such a thing. He didn't know if he was ready to tell Will everything yet. He wasn't sure he could get his own head around the loss he felt in his bones and the fear that Anya could expose them.

"Nice subject change. What happened?" he insisted.

"It's a long story," Matt said, shaking his head.

"Will…I mean *Matt,* fell in love with the reporter assigned to find some dirt on the band," Miles said.

"That doesn't sound like a long story, to be honest," Will said.

"Natasha and she…" Matt began.

"Anya," Miles said with a grin.

Matt threw him some shade. "Natasha and Anya…"

"Yeah, I know. I've been holed up in Hanging On with Natasha all afternoon getting reacquainted with her. She texted me as soon as she was fired. Well, I assume she thought she was texting you…but still. I know everything. Maybe more than you do. I just wanted to watch you squirm," Will said.

"You do not know more than me. And how the hell did Natasha have your number?" Matt said, anger tweaking his misery.

Will hesitated. "Oh right. Oh *right.* Was that weird? I forgot to tell you that me and Natasha had a little thing going before my accident." He pulled an apologetic face.

"That's why she was so strange around me? You dick. How could you forget to tell me that?"

"I was high," Will said.

"You can't use that as an excuse for everything, dude," Matt said. "Besides, we've got bigger problems now."

"I think you're missing the point here," Will said. "I had time to think while I was away. Guys, listen. We're multi-million dollar artists. This whole tour—and the livelihood of LJ and his company and the whole crew—is dependent on us right now. If not now, when can we ever make demands? When can we take charge? When can we insist on not letting terrorists like Paige win? They can't just fire our friends. We're American. We must not let terrorists win, dammit."

Miles raised his hand.

"Yeah, I know Miles. You're British, but you're supposed to be shoulder to shoulder with us when it comes to terrorists."

"I am. Paige scares the crap out of me," Miles said wincing.

"And let's not forget that she's had her tongue in your mouth, too," Ryder said.

"Did she? I wiped it from my memory. Deleted." Miles shuddered and grabbed his phone.

"So what are you suggesting, Will?" Trevin asked.

"Just that we shouldn't stand by and let one of our opening acts get our friends fired. We want Anya and Natasha around, we should be able to have them around. Who's with me?"

Everyone raised their hands.

"Wait, wait, wait," Matt said "Hold on. What do you mean 'getting our friends fired?' It was just Natasha that got fired, wasn't it? I mean, Anya will just go back to WowSounds, right?"

Will frowned. "I doubt it. Natasha told me that Anya was expelled from the tour. And probably fired from the magazine, too."

"No…" Matt murmured. That couldn't be, could it?

How could she have walked out after their first fight? Who *did* that?

Will nudged him. "I need to talk to you. You and I have something to discuss. Speak to you outside?" Will got up and saw the PC on the table. "Wait, you guys haven't taken to watching porn together since I've been gone, have you? Not sure I can buy into that."

Nathan hit a button, and a girl's voice came flooding out of the speakers. He was still watching that one video she'd posted.

"Who's singing our song?" Will asked.

"Just a girl in her bedroom," Nathan said, shrugging. His eyes were on the screen again. "Abby, it says her name is."

"Huh. Nice voice."

Nathan just nodded. "Nice everything."

Matt followed Will out of the bus, wondering what he wanted to talk about.

As soon as the door closed, Will dived straight in. "Look, there's no way to sugarcoat this. How into this Anya are you?"

"Very." *What in the hell was he getting at*?

"Natasha texted me as soon as she was fired, and I got here as soon as I could. She wasn't worried about herself, she was worried about Anya."

"Why?"

"Well, aside from the fact that it was Natasha who took

the dress and put Anya in Paige's sights, she told me that Anya doesn't have anywhere to go. She's been homeless since she was fifteen. Her mom ran off and left her."

The bottom fell out of Matt's world. Why hadn't she told him? How was it possible that he didn't know? Where in hell was she now? Why hadn't she trusted him?

Maybe because I didn't trust her.

"You didn't tell her who you were, so you can't have expected her to trust you when you didn't trust her," Will said, uncannily reading his mind as he'd always done. And then he punched him firmly on the arm.

"What the hell, man?" Matt said, rubbing his bicep.

"That's from Natasha. She says you're so dumb for thinking Anya would write anything to hurt you. Is she right?"

Matt's gaze rested on the place he'd last seen her, between the bus and the gate. Hell, she hadn't even grassed Natasha up for the dress. She'd allowed him to believe it was Anya who'd taken it. He clenched his fists. "Yeah, she probably is."

"How long has it been since you last saw her?"

Matt looked at his watch and his stomach clenched. "Nearly six hours."

"Did you leave on good terms?"

He gritted his teeth, remembering how cold he'd been to her. "No."

"And there have been no blog posts, no Tweets, no articles, no teasers of a huge story?"

"No." *Fuck. What have I done?*

"What do I do?" Matt grabbed Will's shirt in his fists and yanked it. "What do I do? How can I find her?" All he could feel was fire in his belly and heat in his face. He gritted his teeth again, this time not in anger, but trying really hard not to cry like a fucking baby.

"Firstly, get your hands off my wife-beater, you'll pull it out of shape. Secondly, we'll find her. Don't worry about that. We have the attention of the world's media if we want it. So take a chill pill—"

Matt let go of his shirt. "Another rehab joke?"

"Kinda." Will looked at his watch. "I'm going to go get Natasha. Take a few minutes and come up with a way to make things right with Anya when we find her. How to get her off the street and look after her, okay? I'll be back in ten." He checked his watch again and smiled. "Maybe twenty."

"We only have forty minutes to showtime," Matt called as he watched him go, a million confusing feelings fighting for dominance. Knowing Anya was on the street, knowing she hadn't betrayed them, seeing his brother again and knowing he'd have to leave the tour, wondering how to find Anya…

He shook his head and went up the trailer steps, his hand trembling as he opened the door.

Ten minutes later, Matt was standing in the corner and Will and Natasha were snuggled up on the sofa of The One.

"This is all kinds of wrong, man," Miles said. "There shouldn't be chicks on the bus."

"Pot, meet the kettle. Kettle, meet the pot," Ryder said, barely taking his eyes off the TV screen.

"That was different. You were all asleep," Miles said, his eyes lighting up, obviously remembering that night he'd spent with Aimee.

And that made Matt think about spending the night with Anya in her bus. And that amazing, sexy, comfortable night under the stars.

He shifted his weight from one foot to the other. He was on hold, waiting for the manager of the shelter in Tulsa to come to the phone. The manager knew Anya and was the best way of getting in contact with her. As the hold-music hymn played, he tried to keep track of the conversation in the bus.

"I'll be gone in a few minutes, I promise." Natasha turned to Will and grinned. "I am so happy you're here. I was seriously considering a laxative punishment for you blanking me and moving on to Anya with absolutely no acknowledgment of that night we spent—"

"Ahem," Will cut her off. "You can punish me later for that. So do we have a plan?"

"Well, yes. We fire the merry band of monsters, Cherry, and insist that Natasha gets her job back," Miles said. "But that doesn't cover the most important part, does it? No offense," he said, looking at Natasha.

"None taken. I agree that finding Anya takes priority. I can't bear the thought of her alone on the streets." Natasha said.

"I've been in some horrible places when I was younger, and I'm telling you, it's no picnic out there. Finding her is our first priority. Will? I mean Matt?" Miles frowned and shook his head at his slipup.

Matt was in the kitchen on his second hymn as he listened to the guys talk. Emotion rose in his throat when he realized he wasn't alone in this. That he and Will weren't alone here. These guys were family. Real family.

The woman came back on the phone, and he held up his finger as he spoke. "That's great. Right, hang on."

He drew in air, asking someone for something to write with, and Nathan slid a comic book and a pen over to him.

"Thanks. Thank you." He hung up. "I've got their address. The shelter manager wasn't there, but she said she'd keep an eye out for Anya. The best news is that a friend of hers has been staying there, so she thinks Anya might be on her way there. I'm going to try her boss at WowSounds, just in case they didn't fire her."

He keyed in the phone number he'd gotten from the WowSounds site and asked to speak to the editor. After identifying himself as Will, the conversation progressed much quicker.

Still, it took a few minutes for him to convince the receptionist that this wasn't a joke. Yes, he needed to know where Anya was.

Unfortunately, she barely had more information than he did. Apparently she'd covered her tracks too well. And yes, she'd been fired for failing to file a story. Beyond that, the receptionist had no further information. But she wanted an autograph, which Matt promised her.

He hung up.

"They only have an email address for her that they wouldn't give me. They sent a check to her at an address in Tulsa, but that turned out to be a grocery store."

He wanted to say why she'd been fired, but he didn't want Natasha to gloat, or to remind himself that he'd thought that she might betray them.

"Do you have a photo of her?" Will asked.

Matt pulled up the photo he'd sneaked when he'd been in the makeup chair the night before. Shit, had he only been without her one day?

Trevin stood up. "Okay, enough. We have a show to do." He held up his hand to Matt, who started to protest. "I know she means a lot to you, but there are twenty thousand people here who've paid to see you perform. So we do our show."

Matt looked at Will, uncertain if he wanted to get onstage again.

"I'm sorry," Will said. "I can't do the show cold like that. Maybe after a couple of days of watching. I'd balls it all up if I went on now."

"Fine," Trevin said. "I'm sure Matt can pull off one more show for us."

"One condition," Matt said.

Trevin coughed hard, like he was choking. "And what's that?"

Matt looked at Will silently. Will nodded.

"Shit. Are you two telepathic?" Nathan asked, looking like he'd seen Will levitate.

"Tele-pathetic, more like," Ryder grumbled.

"Just tell me what this 'one condition' is," Trevin said.

Matt squared his shoulders. "After the show, we *all* go look for her. Deal?"

Trevin looked bewildered. "Of course we're all going with you. Why would you think we wouldn't? Right, guys? We're family."

A chorus of agreement and chops-busting seemed to rock the whole coach. Matt bit his lip and turned away to rearrange the knives and forks in the sink. As soon as he had his shit together again, he turned back to his friends—no, his *family*.

Natasha stood. "Hey, if you're all going, I'm going. She trusted me with her secret, and I'm not going to let you guys barrel in and do something stupid." She looked at Matt. "No offence, I know you're her boyfriend, but I also know you guys."

For the first time that day, Matt smiled. Boyfriend. Hell yeah. He was her boyfriend.

"Let's hit it. You guys ready?" Trevin looked at Matt, Nathan, Ryder, and Miles in turn. "We'll deal with LJ and Cherry together once we've found Anya."

"Absolutely," Ryder said as the others nodded. "I can't wait for that part."

Chapter Nineteen

They made great time after the show. Matt had never seen the guys move to fast. The second they finished their last number, they ran back to The One, where Natasha had snacks and drinks already prepped for the journey.

Their plan was to scout the city, each taking a different area, and then to meet up at the bus station. Natasha had started making calls during the concert and had found out there'd been a bus leaving for Tulsa via Dallas a few hours earlier.

With luck, they could either catch up with it—although Matt had zero clue how you could legit flag down a bus if you weren't the police—or make their way to that shelter in Tulsa.

Matt was in the SUV with Nathan, who was doing who-knew-what with his phone. "You're not watching *The Tudors*, are you?" Matt asked, only half joking.

"Seriously? I'm pulling up a map of New Orleans, so I

can direct you up and down the streets. Make sure we don't miss any."

Matt sighed. "Thanks. I have a feeling, though, that she's not here. I think she would have made a run for Tulsa. It's what I'd have done, given the circumstances."

"You mean if you were homeless, had been set up by Paige Parker, fired from your job, and then got caught in a huge thunderstorm?"

"Do a runner? Too right I would." At least, that's what he hoped she'd do. She'd be safe and dry on the bus, and she knew people in Tulsa.

God, please let her be safe.

He gripped the steering wheel like his life depended on it. He just needed to find her.

His phone buzzed and the display showed "Miles." He hit the button to turn on the speaker.

"Yup?"

"Nothing here, mate. I'm sorry. We checked all the shelters in our area and then cruised the streets. I was afraid Ryder might find a new Candy Cane, ya know? Ow!"

"She was a stripper, not a hooker," he heard Ryder mumble in the background.

Matt grinned in spite of himself. Candy Cane had been an old friend of Ryder's. "Okay, thanks guys. Let's get to the bus station."

Their search came up empty, too. Now it was down to only Will and Natasha.

By the time Matt and Nathan got there, Natasha was jumping up and down with barely concealed excitement.

"What have you got?" Matt asked.

"A driver in the office remembered her trying to get on

a bus he was getting out of. But he's sure she got on it with the new driver. I asked at the reservation desk, and he said she bought a ticket to Tulsa on the bus that went through Dallas. I'm sure it's her. When we talked, she definitely said she'd have to get a bus back to Tulsa if she lost her job. It's her. I'm sure of it."

Her eyes sparkled, and Matt suddenly knew what his brother saw in her. Maybe he *and* his brother might both get a happily ever after out of this.

He reached through his window and put his hand on hers. "Thank you. You coming with us?"

"Hells yeah. We all are. We're just waiting for you to take the lead."

"On it," Matt said.

She nodded at him, smiling, and ran back to Will's SUV.

"Can you put in the shelter name and get us directions?" he asked Nathan.

Nathan shook his phone at him. "Already there. It'll take ten hours. But I bet you can do it faster." He grinned and raised his eyebrows.

"Bet your ass I can. Buckle up!" Matt shifted into drive and passed the others slowly, watching as they fell into line behind him.

• • •

It was nearly five a.m. when Anya arrived at St John's in the Vale shelter. She thought she'd never get dry again. She'd sat on two buses, damp and miserable, for nearly twenty hours. She'd tried to sleep. After all, she was safe on the bus. But sleep wouldn't come.

All she kept thinking of was Matt. How he hated her.

The whole time she'd been sitting on the story of a lifetime. But some things were more important than money… no matter how desperately you needed it.

What would she do now? Could she write anymore? She wouldn't. Not if writing meant hurting someone. She didn't even know if she could. Writing had been an escape for her, a way to get out of herself and her situation. But then it had been about money. And now she had so many feelings, she would never be able to write them down. She hadn't even looked at her notebook since Matt had given it back. Hadn't even touched it after she put it away. She had no words anymore.

Jude was at St. Johns, asleep. Father Howard pointed him out to her. As usual, he'd moved his cot out of line so that he could sleep with his back to the corner of the wall.

Father Howard led her to his office, where she'd been a few short days before.

"What happened?" he asked. "I thought you'd be there for a few weeks."

She dug her hands into her jacket pocket and pulled out the remaining cash. It was damp from the rain. She put it on his desk. "They thought I stole something, so they asked me to leave."

His eyebrows shot into his hair. "And did you?"

"No. I mean, I don't know. I wore a dress someone gave me, but I'm not sure she was supposed to give it to me." She shoved her hands over her face. She couldn't believe she was having to confess her sins before she'd even taken off her jacket.

"And what about that young man you left with?"

"He thinks I stole the dress…probably. I don't know," she wailed, head still in her hands. "It doesn't even matter. He thinks I broke his trust."

"You like him?"

"I *liked* him." She sniffed and raised her head. "But that doesn't matter now. I'm back. And I wondered if you'd let Jude and me stay a bit longer, if I give you the money I made. I think I just need some time to find a job and to persuade him to get help. How is he?"

Father Howard smiled. "He's good. He was at the veteran's hospital. That's why you couldn't find him. He's got a long way to go, but he's better. But also, Anya—and this is very important to hear—he is not your responsibility. I'm going to look after him. The last couple of days he's been helping out here, and I think he's going to be a great asset to us reaching out to other homeless veterans on the street."

Relief washed over her. "Really? He's doing well? That's—" She swallowed. "That's such good news." Now she needed to sleep and try to figure out where *she* fit in. What she could do. She stood and grabbed her backpack. "May I go find a cot?"

He leaned back in his chair. "I don't think so, Anya. It might be better if you found somewhere more permanent to stay, don't you think?"

She slumped. Of course. It was probably full. She hadn't even thought. But it was raining so hard. "Of course, Father. But could I maybe sleep on the floor, just for tonight? I promise I'll leave in the morning."

"Anya, I think you're misunderstanding me. I've been talking to… Maybe you need a moment?" He moved his eyes toward the door that led to the church side of the building.

He wanted her to talk to God?

"Okay..." She dropped her backpack again and opened the door.

The church was ablaze with light, and after the dimness of the shelter and the lamplight in Father Howard's office, it took her eyes a moment to adjust.

What?

She looked back into his office. He was suppressing a smile and tapping a yellow pencil against his nose, trying, she assumed, to look innocent.

Chapter Twenty

"Anya!"

Her heart quickened even before she registered the voice. She blinked several times in the brightness of the lights. A figure came out of the glare.

"Will? Or…" she asked, squinting.

"Matt," he said.

She closed her eyes and shook her head, half wondering if she was dreaming.

"Open your eyes," he said.

She did. And there he was. Really real. In front of her. Looking—she swallowed hard—like a dream. She stretched out her hand to poke him. Just to check if he was really, really real. "Matt?"

"Yes. I'm sorry. Sorry for everything. But yes, it's Matt."

"You're here?" One of the lights in the church was buzzing, or maybe it was just in her head.

"Say my name again," he whispered.

"Matt." She paused. "You *are* Matt, aren't you?"

"I am." His eyes glassed over, like he was holding back. "I'm so sorry for being an ass, for lying to you about my name. Will had a big problem that he needed to take care of, and the only option was for me to take his place. I wouldn't have lied to you, but LJ would have sued Will and my mom if he left the tour to get help. I couldn't let that happen." He swallowed visibly and lowered his voice. "I thought I'd lost you forever."

"You're damn right he's sorry. He sang off-key all bloody night!" Miles said.

She peeked behind Matt and saw them all there, all grinning. Miles, Nathan, Ryder, Trevin, and Natasha. She did a double take. Natasha had her arms around Will. She stole a look back at Matt, and then again at Will. "Wow. I thought I knew…but…"

Matt glanced behind him at Will and smiled. "I know." He took a step forward and gazed into her eyes. Her heart soared as she saw the emotion there. He reached out with one hand and took hers. "You knew, and you didn't go straight to a tabloid? You didn't want to tell the world? You would have made a fortune."

"That's not the kind of writing I want to do, as it turns out," she said simply. "I realized that even before I figured out who you were." Her heart raced being so close to him. "I thought maybe I could, but it turns out, I couldn't."

"Come back with us," Matt said. "Please."

"And do what? I…" She shook her head hopelessly. "I have to find a job and…"

"Listen. My mom's spoken to the priest here. She wants you to come and stay with her until I swap back with Will.

Then all we have to do is get you into college. Father Howard told us he'd already got you through your GED, so there's no excuse. You can go with me if you want. No strings, no pressure, no nothing."

Her voice was close to cracking. The promise was so good, but the reality crumbled under any kind of scrutiny. "I can't afford college. I can't even afford to eat if I'm not here. I can't just freeload at your mom's house. I don't want that."

"Actually, we know how you can pay your own way, right Will?"

Will stepped forward. "Yeah. I read the article you wrote about the homeless in Tulsa. You write with heart, and so simply that even I can understand." He smiled at her, the same way but still different from how Matt smiled at her.

Matt took over. "I've been making calls all the way here. I've promised Rolling Stone an exclusive article about Will coming back from drug addiction. I think you could write our story the right way. And I hear Rolling Stone will pay top dollar. Come back with us. Write our story."

"But won't it get you in trouble if it comes out that you've been taking your brother's place in the band?"

Matt grinned. "I told LJ what I was asking you to do, and that he could either come off as the supportive manager Will didn't want to disappoint, or the manager who got Will hooked on the drugs because 'the band is everything'. Unsurprisingly, he chose the first option. We now have his full support."

An overwhelming wave of emotion surged through her. Could it be possible? Had he really come for her? Searched for her? Made it possible for her to…have a real life?

"Wow, she looks like she's in two minds, dude," Nathan

said. "You must suck at the kissing thing."

No. No he didn't. She leaned forward, but he didn't move toward her. She wanted to kiss him so badly, why wasn't he kissing her already?

And then she realized. She had to go to him. She had to kiss him. He'd come all this way, and now she needed to take the last step. She reached up to his face and touched his cheek. A muscle popped in his jaw as he closed his eyes.

She stepped to him. Everything went silent, everything became Matt. She touched her cheek to his, fluttered her eyelashes against his skin, and then reached for his lips. She brushed hers over his, inhaling his unique smell and relishing in a sensation she hadn't experienced in far too long. Home. He felt like home.

Her tongue touched his bottom lip so very lightly, but that was all it took for him to push his hands into her damp hair. Sparks shot through her body as he kissed her, deeply and hungrily.

When he pulled away, they were both breathing hard. There was a second of silence and then whistles and cheers from the others. He looked around and grinned.

Then without a word, he held out his hand to her, and she took it. He looked at their hands intertwined and love shone from his eyes. And happiness. And everything.

She had everything.

The others left the church, and Matt turned to look at her. He opened his mouth as if to say something, but the door barged open again. It was Will.

"I suppose it's only right, after all this time, that I'm the one to tell you that he loves you, right?" He grinned and let the door close again.

Anya stopped somewhere between shock and amusement. She found it hard to meet Matt's eyes, but he put a hand under her chin and made her.

He held up a finger. "Excuse me for just a moment. I just have to"—he pointed at the door—"kill someone for a second." He shot outside as if he were on fire.

She held a hand against her mouth, not knowing whether to laugh or swoon. Did he really love her? Could he?

A thump followed by an outraged "Ouch!" and Natasha laughing loudly punctuated the silence inside the church.

Matt came back, smoothing down his hair. "Right, where were we?"

"Um..." Anya didn't know what to say, so she just nodded back at the door.

"Oh right. Right. Well, my idiot brother, for once in his life, isn't entirely wrong. But he has no idea—none—about how I feel when you're close to me. How much just being with you lightens me, my mood, my...soul. Shit." He shook his head. "I'm not a poet like Will, but I do love you, Anya Anderson. I may not have the fancy words..."

She put her finger up to his mouth, unable to even put to words the enormity of her emotions. "I'm supposed to be a writer, and I can't even begin..." She swallowed. "I love you right back, Matt Fray. You're home for me."

He squeezed his eyes shut for a second, as if taking in what she'd said. And then he whooped. Loudly. Anya jumped and laughed at the sound echoing around the church. "Yes!" He punched the air, not once, not twice. Anya giggled at his exuberance, hugging herself around the middle as she watched him jump around, fist pumping in a way that the walls of the vestibule had probably never witnessed before.

But then he stopped, planting himself directly in front of her, and looked into her eyes. She reached up and pushed back the hair from his forehead. He closed his eyes again as she touched his face, and then he bent to kiss her. He hesitated for a second with his lips hovering over hers, and then kissed her gently. It was a sweet kiss. It was a perfect kiss. She felt loved. Protected.

And she loved that.

Epilogue

Anya ran to the mailbox and found three letters addressed to her care of Kara Fray, Matt's mother. One was from the state university, one was from Tulsa, and the other was marked "Studio City". She opened the Tulsa one first, as she sat on the porch steps.

Jude was staying permanently at Father Howard's, working at the shelter and helping other war veterans get the care they needed. He sounded good, although he still refused to use a computer in case he was spied on. Maybe that would never go away, but Father Howard had reassured her that he was doing really well. All his issues that made it difficult for him to find regular work made him the perfect person to reach out to other veterans.

A tear squeezed out of one eye as she looked around the front yard. Beautiful tropical flowers grew all around and palm trees dotted the fence line. How was it possible to be so happy, so fortunate?

Matt banged out of the front door. "Everything okay?" He sat next to her.

She swiped at the errant tear. "Jude's doing well. He sounds happy." Anya stuffed the letter back into its envelope. She'd write back this afternoon. She kind of loved the ritual of finding nice paper and writing in longhand. And he always commented on the paper she used, which had made her go out of her way to find interesting stationery to write on.

"Anya. What about the other envelope?" He eyed the one in her lap.

"Which one?" She lifted the smaller one and the large brown envelope from the college.

"You know which I mean."

She hesitated. This was the last piece of the puzzle. The last planet to align. "I can't…"

"Are you being a fraidycat?" He raised his eyebrows.

"Maybe." She sighed. "Everything has been so perfect. Your mom letting me have a room here, you've been so—" Now more than one tear was threatening to fall. He put his arm around her and pressed his lips to her temple. "—annoying." She choked out a laugh. "It seems impossible that they would accept me. That we'd be going to college together. It's too much good stuff to happen at one time to me."

. . .

Matt knew it was an acceptance, because he'd received his earlier in the year before he'd gone on tour. And no university sent a thick package of stuff just to say "We regret to inform you…"

And her essay had been a work of art. She didn't just

edit the Rolling Stone article, although she could have, she didn't replicate her homeless article either, although she could have. She wrote instead about the ways in which allowing herself to trust the people in her life had opened her eyes to the possibilities that lay before her. Had changed her whole world in every way possible. The essay had made him cry when he read it, but that secret he'd take to the grave.

So he'd known, even before the letter came. But he wanted her to believe it could happen. If she didn't, she'd always wonder if everything would fall away as it had so many times before.

"Anya. You deserve this. You know it. You had a chance to make a fortune, but you chose not to because you didn't want to hurt anyone. You've been on the street since you were fifteen, and still your primary concern was a man who helped you there. My mom loves you, and let me tell you— that doesn't happen easily. Although, to be fair, she doesn't know you slip into my room sometimes when she's asleep."

Anya nudged her leg against his in a mild rebuke.

"What I'm saying is that you deserve to go to school. And whether this one school says yes or no, you deserve an education. You deserve great things. Don't ever forget that." He wished that for just one second she could see herself how he saw her, but he was prepared to keep working on that. Miracles didn't happen overnight.

"How *is* Will?" she asked.

"He's fine. They're all fine. Since they confronted LJ about…well, everything, they have much more control. Cherry was fired, the new opening act seems to be working out…and the tour has been revitalized with some new numbers that the guys wanted to add. Now stop changing the subject and open it." He handed it back to her.

She took it, and he swore he saw her hands shake. He wanted to hold her so badly, but she needed to open the damn envelope first.

She tore off the end and took out the clump of brochures and leaflets. "Dear Ms. Anderson. We are delighted to inform you…" Her voice cracked and she started to sob. Like huge, gut-wrenching sobs.

He pulled her onto his lap and wrapped both arms around her. "You made it," he whispered. "You're coming to school with me."

She sniffed and looked at him with her beautiful dark eyes. "*We* made it. I couldn't have done this without you, or Will, or your mom. Thank you."

"You're welcome. Now how about the other letter?"

Her gaze shifted to the other one and she ripped into it through her tears and pulled out a stiff card. "I don't believe…" she started, before peering closer at the invitation in her hand. She rubbed her eyes and read again. "I can't… Rolling Stone nominated my article for an award. They've invited me to an awards dinner."

He wasn't exactly surprised. The article had been syndicated around the world and every news show had covered it.

"You wrote a great article, sweetheart. Everyone thought so. They'll probably make a movie about it."

She just looked at him, and he never wanted her to stop looking at him like that, with eyes pooled with happiness.

He kissed her and then stood with her still in his arms. She shrieked and laughed as he spun with her.

He loved hearing her laugh.

Loved.

Acknowledgments

I'd like to thank Ophelia London, Lisa Burstein, Rebekah L Purdy and Erin Butler for allowing me to a part of this fun boyband ride! Also huge thanks go to Heather Howland (as usual) and to Stephen Morgan, editor extrordinaire— hopefully (for me at least) this is just the first of many!

And last but not least, my husband, whose support is an incalculable factor in me being able to write at all. I love you.

About the Author

Suze Winegardner is an editor and a romance writer. An expat Brit, she quells her homesickness with Cadbury Flakes and Fray Bentos pies. She's lived in London, Paris, and New York, and now lives exactly where the military tells her to. When not writing, Suze loves to travel with her active-duty husband and take long walks with their Lab. All things considered, her life is chock full of hoot, just a little bit of nanny. And if you get that reference…well, she already considers you kin.

Made in the USA
Lexington, KY
16 August 2015